I0822379

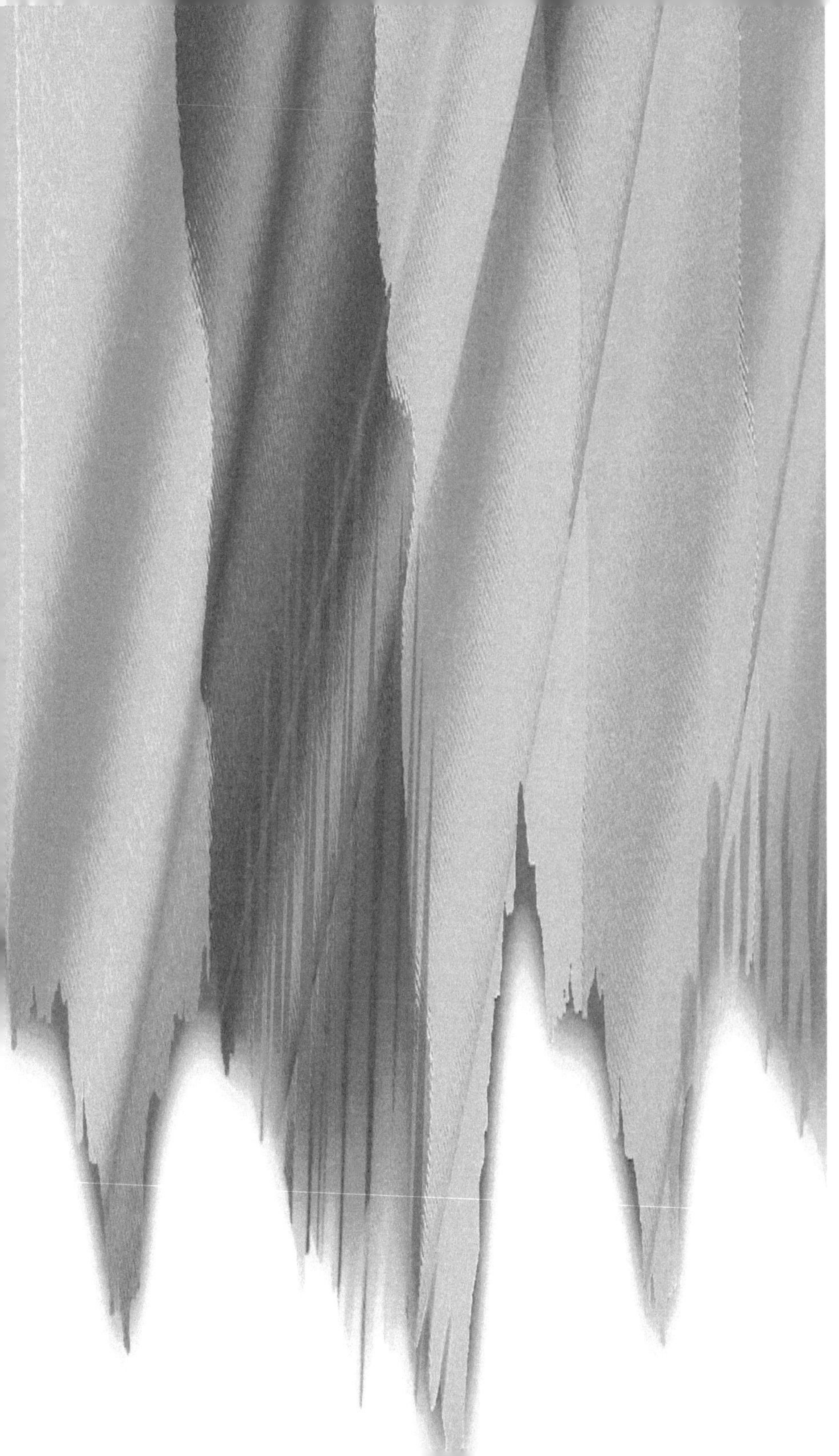

Chevel Nelson
New York, NY

Author's Note: This is a work of fiction. Names, characters, places, and incidents are a product of the author's imagination. Locales and public names are sometimes used for atmospheric purposes. Any resemblance to actual people, living or dead, or to businesses, companies, events, institutions, or locales is completely coincidental.

My Gay Ain't Happy/ Chevel Nelson – 2nd ed.
ISBN 979-8-9857104-1-0

Dedication to all my angels that pushed me to complete this work of art and have supported me through it all.

"What I know is that it's going to be better, if it's bad, it might get worse, but I know that it's going to be better. And you have to know that. No matter how dull and seemingly unpromising life is right now, it's going to change. It's going to be better.

But you have to keep working."

- Maya Angelou

Contents

Patrick

Ever see those old Charlie Brown cartoons? You know the ones where the adults sound like Womp, Womp, Womp. That's how I feel every time this doctor opens his mouth to talk. I just feel numb. I am sitting here in this doctor's office not hearing anything he is saying. All I remember hearing is that somehow, I am HIV positive. I am still trying to wrap my head around how that is possible. I don't use drugs, I'm not promiscuous and I haven't given or received any tainted blood. I have been in a committed relationship for the past ten years with Matthew. My dearest Matthew, the love of my life. This is the man I want to grow old with. The man I want to adopt my children with. This man is everything.

How can I tell him?

What will I tell him?

Would he leave me? Would he stay? Would he even believe me if I said I had no idea how I contracted the disease?

I began to shake my head as if to clear out the voices in my head. I had to listen and pay attention to the doctor. How did my routine physical turn into THIS?

Okay, Okay pay attention Patrick, he might be saying something important. The doctor continued to speak. "As I was saying Patrick, people have been living longer and longer with HIV. They just must maintain a healthy lifestyle and keep up on their medicine schedule. There are many good antiretroviral therapy drugs out now, so HIV is not a death sentence like before. There are also new drugs out that make HIV undetectable. It is highly suggested you notify all your sexual partners." Dr. Wu said. Hell, that will be easy I thought, there is only one. "Also, there is actually a positive to your case..." How is there a positive to being HIV positive I thought? "The person that infected you is already on an antiretroviral therapy, so it should make it easier to narrow down who gave it to you. A trace of the drugs showed in testing."

WAIT, WHAT? I thought.

WTF did that mean.

It can't possibly mean what I think it means, that means Matt is HIV positive and he gave it to me.

Dr. Wu kept talking but all I heard again was the Charlie Brown cartoon parents saying "Womp, Womp, Womp, Womp". I started shaking my leg under the table just itching to be anywhere but here. It felt as if steam was coming out of the top of my shirt. All I could think is I have to get out of here. "Thank you, Dr. Wu,", I said as I stood up cutting him off. "Can I have a few days and give you a call before we begin treatment?" I asked. "Sure" Dr. Wu said, "Just make a follow-up appointment at the front desk so we can get started." "Thank you, Dr. Wu." I shook his hand and prepared to leave. Dr. Wu handed me some pamphlets and left the room. I walked out the room after him and politely took my ass past the front desk and didn't stop to make an appointment. I just didn't feel like dealing right now. I'm not sure what I want or need to do next.

Maybe I should go to Matt's job and curse his ass out. No, I should call his mama and tell her what a scumbag her son is and what he did to me. No, Patrick don't you dare drop to his level. One thing I know I wasn't doing was going home. Why should I go to the place where there was once joy and now it was going to be full of pain and lies?

I started walking down the street aimlessly with no destination in mind. All I could do was to wonder why. What did I do to be treated this way? I AM A GOOD FUCKING MAN!!! I know that for certain, I worked hard at it. A faithful man that takes commitment seriously and I thought Matt was also!

He just fucked me with no preparation or lubrication. No fucking foreplay, just dry and dirty.

FUCK!!!

FUCK ME!!!

I threw the damn pamphlets Dr. Wu gave me in the trashcan on the corner. I waited for the streetlight to change, and I noticed there was one pamphlet there for Atripla©.

WAIT A MINUTE!!! I remember I found a triangle pill case like that two weeks ago at home. It was in one of the bags Matt usually takes to the gym. I asked him about the pills, and he said he didn't know where they came from. Said it probably fell in his bag at the gym. He grabbed the triangle from me and threw it out.

That lousy, fucking liar!!!

They were his goddamn pills!

This is all way too much. I know it was only one o'clock in the afternoon, but I needed a drink like yesterday. I just cannot deal with knowing I was in love with a liar and a cheat. I needed an escape and a drink or five was the perfect escape route in this case.

I glanced up and saw there was a bar right across the street from where I stood that was open. Go figure the name of the bar was Nosedive.

How apropos for my situation?

I walked right into the bar to begin my journey of trying to forget my miserable life. The bar was dark just like my mood. This place is perfect right now. It was fairly empty of course since it was early afternoon on a

Wednesday. Looked like it was just the usual neighborhood drunks and me of course with my newly diagnosed diseased ass. One of the greatest perks of being a freelancer was you get to make your own hours. Well, no hours today because the only work I planned on doing was the process of destroying my liver. I needed to contemplate the meaning of my new life.

I chose to sit at a stool at the bar in the far-right corner out of sight and alone. I didn't want to talk to anyone or have any fake pleasantries if necessary. Here I was sitting at the bar with my elbows on the bar and pinching the top of my nose between my eyes. I let out the heaviest sigh. I muttered under my breathe, "I just want this to be all a bad dream and to wake up and laugh." Nervousness made me grab both sides of my short curly hair and hold it in my hands. I was so lost in a trance of disbelief that I forgot where

I was. That was until I heard a sultry baritone voice ask,

"Can I help you with something?"

The mellow smoothness of the voice startled me. I jolted myself out of my self-pity to look up to what could only have been a hallucination. The man standing before me was the most amazing, awe-inspiring creature I have ever seen. I shook my head back and forth quickly. This had to be a dream. No, it was real, HE is real. Again, the man behind the bar asked, "Can I get you something?"

I stuttered and stumbled for what I wanted, sounding like a fool, and asked for a Seven and Seven. The heavenly creature said "Sure" and walked away.

"Um. damn shame." I uttered under my breath. He even looked amazing walking away in his all-black uniform. I just stared at him while he was behind the bar getting my drink. All the delicious and nasty things I could do with and to him. Watching wasn't cheating, hell it wouldn't matter since apparently Matthew cheated, it would just serve him right. No that would solve nothing, but this eye candy was helping to be a welcomed distraction. Adonis returned (that is what I named him in my head because he surely had to be a god looking that damn good) with my drink.

"It must already be a hard day for a Seven and Seven this early" Adonis said. "You have no idea." I replied. "Well, I am all ears if you need a friend." Adonis offered with a full watt smile of straight white teeth. "By way of an introduction, my name is George, let me know if you need anything else. My shift doesn't end until 6pm tonight." "Thanks, I appreciate it." I told him.

George, what an ordinary name for such an exquisite creature. He looked like an Antonio, maybe a Roberto, an Adonis, not a

George. Hell, George was my ugly little brother's name. But this George here.... there wasn't anything ugly about him. He was bronze like he was dipped in gold. His eyes were the most exquisite green and aqua scattered with gold flecks. He had luscious, juicy full lips that looked like they were good for kissing amongst other things. He was chiseled, you could tell how his clothes fit. His body was tight and right, and he looked like his skin was so soft.
I am not sure for what team he played but wherever he played, he most definitely was a starter and star.

As I sipped my drink, shook my head, and thought to myself, "you have enough problems without adding more. Plus, I would never do to anyone else what Matthew did to me. I could never be that trifling. He has now been coined by his government name because of this. Matt was when I was being sweet, Matthew was when I was pissed at him.

Tears started to well in my eyes, how did my life go from wonderful this morning to shit this afternoon? I thought I had found my soul mate and now I am sitting here feeling like a fool. Who is going to want my ass now that I was a contagion?

What in the entire hell!

All of a sudden, a tissue slid next to my hand, and I looked into the most sympathetic eyes. Those damn eyes are hypnotic and just pull you into a trance. I gave a sad smile and with a pitiful cracked voice muttered thank you.

"Things always seem hard during the storm." George said. Hell, he's even compassionate. Oh yeah, my ass was super vulnerable right now. "Just having a moment is all, thanks for being so nice." "Being nice gets me better tips. Only kidding." George chuckled. "Being nice cost nothing and you looked like you could use a little compassion." I genuinely smiled after he said that. It felt good to have someone who didn't know me and who was willing to have compassion.

George walked down to the other end of the bar to assist another sad sap here on a Wednesday afternoon. George. Saying that name made me remember my little brother. I haven't thought of him for a long time and just thinking about him made me realize that I missed him. Our mother had forbidden me to speak to him after I told her I was gay. We were raised by a single mother, and it was just her, me, and my brother George. Our dad decided he no longer wanted to be a father or husband and kind of disappeared when I was around seven. We didn't hear from him after he left. Couldn't even tell you where he was or what he was doing.

Many years ago, when I told my mother I was gay, she politely told me she had no time, energy, or inclination to deal with or raise a gay son. She told me I had to leave. Because me being gay was going to be a bad influence on my little brother and I should start making ways to find a way to live on my own. I know now being from Sumner, Mississippi staying would not be an option. Especially when the most famous thing we were known for was the trial of Emmitt Till's killers. At the time I only had $100 to my name and when I left home, I couldn't even say goodbye, I just left. I made sure I got out of Mississippi quickly and without turning back.

No one wanted to be an openly gay homeless boy in rural Mississippi.

With my little $100 I took a bus and came to New York City. Life in the Big Apple was not easy, but I was determined to make it work. At least I wasn't the only gay boy in New York. What I did not expect was that leaving home would leave me confused and depressed. It made me feel like I did something wrong by being gay. I tried to deny it and to become "straight' but it wasn't as simple as that. I never felt like I belonged back home and most days I felt alone and misunderstood.

In New York I had nowhere to stay so most nights I would fall asleep on a bench at the pier. At the pier I gained friends, and we would hustle and steal in order to eat. We became a community. There were also times I had to do things I am still not proud to even admit. Eventually I could not stay on the piers anymore because cops would come and harass us there. Most would poke us with their batons and others would ask for special "favors". "Favors" were code for blow jobs and after they would get off, they would ridicule you and call you a homo or a fucking faggot. All depended on how much in denial they were on that day.

The cops would say they weren't gay, but the truth was they were repeated customers for my and the other kid's services. Sometimes even after you rendered your services, they would still kick you off the pier. It was like they didn't want to face their shame or truth, I guess. That was the most demeaning part of it all, but you do what you need to do in order to survive. I was and am determined to survive.

Eventually when I became tired enough, I ended up at Safe Haven. Safe Haven was where all the homeless or runaway kids eventually went. At that time, it was on teens all the way west in the city. Couldn't tell you if it was better or worse than the piers. It was trading one bad situation for another. The only difference was either you slept in a bed or on a bench. At Safe Haven you didn't have to worry about the cops, but you did have to worry about robbing and stealing. Oh and of course the sex, both wanted and unwanted. Sex at Safe Haven was more of the ganging up variety as opposed to the simple blow job at the piers. No one enjoys a gang rape or train as they would call it. The only train I enjoyed being on was the A train to Far Rockaway when I was trying to escape my nightmares. The first day I arrived I was told when I walked in, I had to make a choice. Either I choose a gang or become somebody's bitch.

Neither choice was very appealing to me.

Not even the staff cared. They were just there for a job and could care less what went on. It was like every man was for himself especially when it came time for curfew, and you had to be in by 9 o'clock. After the lights went out it became free for all until the morning.

Wow, those was crazy times.

That is where I met David. David and I become our own two-person gang. David would have you believe he was soft or a punk but a punk he was not. David was an uncover thug and try him if you wanted to and you would definitely lose. David had it harder than me because David is gorgeous. Almost as gorgeous as Adonis here. They had almost the same kind of eyes and skin tone. The only difference was the cooper flecks Adonis has in his eyes. Other difference was that David was Indian. Not Native American but Indian from India. Most people thought he was Puerto Rican and would often walk up to him and start speaking in Spanish. We would crack up behind that. Yeah, I really miss David.

I heard he is in the ballroom scene now. That really wasn't my thing, and I haven't been to a ball in years. I know that David is doing well, he had the same hustler mentality I did. New York has a way of bringing it out in you. If you wanted to survive you had to know how to hustle or you would starve or be eaten alive by these streets. New York was not for the faint of heart.

Hell, anyone would be doing well with a face like that. He could easily become a model just life has a tendency to get in the way. David could scrap and was not afraid to go toe to toe with anyone. One would think he would be worried about messing up his face, but he could care less. Yeah, that was my only friend, and we became thick as thieves. We would always find a way to get money. We could either be found singing and dancing in the train stations or drawing cartoons of people in Central Park. We would do whatever it took to make a little bit of a change to get something to eat or to buy ourselves some clothing.

I have always been good at drawing and David was an amazing singer and dancer. We made pretty decent money when we weren't struggling by homeless boy standards. After several years both David and I wanted more. We both just wanted different things,

David wanted to perform, and I wanted to explore the opportunity to draw and design. David eventually left and I applied to Parsons. Got a full scholarship because I put down, I was an orphan since basically I was, at least in New York. I ended up becoming a design artist after two years and after that I started working full time.

When David left Safe Haven, we lost touch. Without David I just couldn't live there anymore. So, after my first check, I immediately moved out of Safe Haven and found a room in one of the brownstones nearby. It was an old elderly couple that rented it and I stayed there for a few years before getting my own apartment.

Found out that they changed the old Safe Haven into a hotel and club. Oh, the secrets that place could tell if it spoke.

Anyway, I began working as an intern at this designer shop, when one day this good-looking rugged gentleman came in to drop off some supplies that we needed to model a kitchen for one of our fancy clients. I checked him out, but I wasn't sure if he was straight or gay, so I was very cautious. I didn't need to lose my job over a crush. I approached him and sparked an easy conversation that ended up lasting an hour. He was really easy to talk to and extremely easy on the eyes. He also had an amazing spirit and told me his name was Matthew or Matt for short. We just bonded and every time he dropped off supplies, he would make an effort to have a conversation with me and of course I made it my point to make sure that I was the one there to assist him.

We became fast friends I got to know him, and I liked him a lot as a person. I didn't and still don't have many friends, so it was the highlight of my week to see and speak to him. During one of the holidays, he asked me if I was going home to be with family and I was honest and told him my story about my mother not wanting a gay son. Something about him made me trust him. Matt was a sweetheart and invited me over to dinner one evening with his family. His family dynamic was so different than what I was accustomed to or had ever seen. His parents were supportive of him being gay and encouraged him to live his truth. They were there whenever he needed them. It was amazing to see that level of support. We started becoming best friends and I got to know him and all of his family really well.

It felt good to be part of something and eventually we ended up falling in love. I think we fell in love before our first kiss and that first kiss and first-time making love was amazing. We both had had sexual experiences, but it was something about our connection that felt so very right. That connection made me feel like I could feel him in my soul, and he said he could imagine me in his. I started to really fall in love with this man and until today it has been the best ten years of our lives.

There were occasional arguments but that is what couples have but nothing big enough to ever put a wedge between us. Actually, we only had one huge fight about six months ago. It was our first and only fight ever. Otherwise, things would have been great, almost blissful. Now there was this.

I don't know if this is a forgivable offense or if this is a deal breaker. I don't know if I could ever forgive him. I mean the bartender is kind of cute. George is very sweet and kind of flirty.

That would definitely not solve any problems. At the end of the day, I would still be diseased.

I know Matthew and I have to have a conversation sooner rather than later. What do I say to him? How can I not be angry at him for blowing up our lives, our dreams? This might be more than one conversation. How do I handle it? Do come in hot with motherfucker this, and saying motherfucker what the fuck?

What did I do to deserve this?

How could you not tell me?

How could you lie?

An omission of the truth is a lie by pure definition. He omitted to tell me that he was HIV positive, and he put me in harm's direct way. I don't know what I'm going to do.

I wish I could call someone, maybe my friend Xiomara. No, Xiomara wouldn't be able to help. She is going through her own self identity crisis. One minute she's a lesbian, the next she is straight. I really like her friend Amanda though. Amanda definitely deserved better than Xiomara and all of her continuing drama. No, the only person I needed to speak to was Matthew.

What I do know is right now, I'm gonna sit here with these fellow drunks and I'm going to keep drinking and keep flirting with this Adonis. Flirting was as far as it is going to go. I refuse to put anyone in the situation I am in and who besides Matthew's ass is going to want someone with these scarlet letters on my chest called HIV.

I really just wanted my mom. Who is going to want to be with me? Who is going to want to love me? Can I even start a family and adopt the kids I so desperately wanted? I wanted a family; I deserved a family. All I was feeling right now was like that rejected little boy. The little boy his mama didn't want because he was gay. I thought I had a man who adored me but apparently, I was not enough. Matthew doesn't love me or want me how could he and cheat on me.

He damn sure doesn't respect me, If he did, he would not have done what he did to me or at the very least used a condom if he was going to cheat.

Sitting here crying in this glass at the bar was not helpful at all. These tears won't help anything. These tears won't make it better. These tears won't heal me. I will forever have the letters HIV listed next to my name.

How do you move forward through the trenches when all you want to do is lay down and die?

How would I ever be able to look at Matthew the same after he has hurt me like he has?

What I do know is I need to get out of this bar because it is now almost five o'clock. I couldn't live here and eventually had to go home. I am not sure how to start this conversation, but hell by the end of it all, Matthew will feel my wrath.

He is going to get a full dictionary of words and some words that aren't even in the dictionary. He will know the level of hurt and disappointment I have in my heart. He will know how I feel, like he threw away our dream. How he threw away my security. How he threw away me and my heart. How he took it all and treated it like a doormat. How he was selfish and had me wondering if he was ever telling me the truth. Where was he all those times, he wasn't home. Were you really visiting your friends and family or out having sex with someone else?

Did you ever really love me, or did you just feel sorry for the poor little, pitiful boy whose mother could not deal with the fact that he was gay? The same mother that left me to navigate this world all by myself.

I am not sure if there are any answers to these questions, but I am sure as hell planned to find out. Forrest Gump told us a lie. Our lives were not like he promised, there was no box of chocolate anywhere in sight. It was just rotten lemons that posed as sweet lemonade. As soon as I had this thought my phone began to buzz.

Of course, it was Matthew probably wondering why I wasn't at home to greet him. Well, he can wait like he waited to tell me he had HIV. I sent his call to voicemail. He then just kept calling so I turned my phone off. I didn't want to go home but I knew I had to. We had to have a face-to-face conversation. As I got up to pay my bill and prepared to walk home all I could think of was tonight about to be a very interesting evening.

CHAPTER TWO- THE REPENTANT ONE

Matt

I fucked up something horrible. Some way, somehow, I have to figure this all out. I definitely owe Patrick a conversation and an explanation before he finds out. It was a stupid, stupid mistake and now it is a mistake, I have to live for the rest of my life. I have been hiding my medicines at work, so he won't suspect anything but eventually I have to come clean. How could I have been so stupid!! For one night, six months ago, it all changed. My happy life turned to shit. Doesn't matter how mad I was or how good the sex was, I am about to throw away ten years together because of it. We just got married a few years ago because it was finally legal in our state. We were talking about starting a family and adopting kids and now that might not be an option. We might not be an option.

Damn, here comes Justin. I really hate this dude, but he is the owner and I need my job, so I have to play nice. He just irks me because he is always flirting knowing I have a husband. I guess I should be flattered although I am far from it. I just wanted to figure out how things got so very bad at home. I just want everything to be back to the way it used to be between Patrick and me. When we were laughing and loving one another. When arguments were far and few between. When I was faithful. When I was not HIV positive.

"Hello Justin, I am fine. Yes, I am still married. Yes, I am still happy thanks for asking. You have a good day too." When will he catch a hint or buy a clue that I am not at all interested in him? He is like a greedy kid in a candy store. He wants it all and he wants it now, no matter who gives it. Justin is an equal opportunity type of guy. It doesn't seem to matter if it is she/he/they or them, he is down for whatever. That wasn't me. I loved stability and that is what Patrick provides. I wish I knew what I know now. Alcohol in a bar and hurt feelings do not make for the best of bed fellows. That is how I ended up in this predicament I'm in. I really, really fucked up so very badly. I love Patrick, I promise you I do. I do admit I did partake in a one-night stand sixth months ago and this is my reward, HIV. I remember perfectly when it happened, we had had a massive argument.

Thinking back, I can't even remember what we were arguing about, but we said some pretty hurtful things to one another. Instead of putting my hands on him, I decided to leave and get some air. Thought things would be better once we both cool off. I was walking around, and I ended up at this whole in the wall bar.

The bartender was gorgeous. He was so handsome I can't even explain what he looked like. Just gorgeous with the most beautiful eyes and the nicest smile. And so very nice to me. He made me feel like I was wanted. I felt handsome around him. Patrick didn't make me feel handsome anymore. I think Patrick had just gotten comfortable with me. Gotten used to our lives and just didn't see me anymore.

Think we have been together so long that we forgot to give one another those little nuances. We very rarely say I love you or tell each other how handsome the other was. I missed the days when he would tell me I looked good that day, especially when he knew how hard it was to work at my job. Patrick knew all about Justin and his constant uncomfortable flirting. It wasn't that way when Justin's dad ran the company and I have been constantly thinking about changing jobs. We always spoke about Justin being a piece of work.

That's neither here nor there. I do remember I was pretty drunk that night. Combined with the bartender flirting, I was feeling good. Feeling wanted and needed which I haven't felt in such a long time. Ended up staying at the bar until closing time. Instead of the bartender asking me to leave like he did the other patrons, he just locked the door and let me sit there. He then came over and whispered in my ear which sent jolts down my spine. I was excited because he was sexy as hell, and he chose me out of everyone in the bar. He said his name was G and he proceeded to clean the bar and flirt as I sat there nursing a glass of water. G came over and rubbed the back of his hand down the side of my face. I shivered. He then asked me if I felt like having a good time. All thoughts about Patrick left my head. All I could see was this sexy man courting me. I do remember telling him that I didn't have much time and he said no worries.

We ended up in some little motel not far from the bar. We had a great time that evening. The sex was unbelievable and directly afterwards, the guilt set in.

What did I just do?

I then realized I didn't use protection. Patrick and I have been together so long that protection was never an issue. Who would've thought a couple of hours would lead me to where I am right now? That a few hours meant that I would be damaged for the rest of my life.

I went home afterwards and slept in the guest bedroom after I showered. Patrick was already asleep, and I wanted no questions or arguments. The next morning, we were back to normal as if nothing happened. Patrick had made breakfast and kissed me to apologize. It was just a regular old day, nothing special, nothing new. We just chilled out and enjoyed each other's company.

Everything eventually went back to normal except for my guilt. I was fine. I promise you it was all be fine for a while. It was just me and Patrick. I didn't think about anything or anyone else. I recommitted myself to us. That was until I saw a sore on my hip.

I didn't remember hitting my side but went to the doctor anyway because the sore became itchy, and I didn't want to scratch it. When I went to the doctor, he suggested a blood test. Couldn't understand why but that is how I found out the scar was actually an HIV lesion. The doctor offered information and gave me all these pamphlets and a trial pack of a medication called Atripla©. There was only one person I could have got it from, and it was G. I went to the bar to tell him about me being positive and he showed genuine concern and said he would get tested.

I couldn't tell Patrick about this when I found out. Things were going really well with us. I was biding my time to let him know. Maybe just being a coward. Whatever the case I had to protect Patrick at all costs.

I was working long hours in order to avoid Patrick. Just didn't want him to get sick, he didn't deserve it. It was not easy I did what I had to do. Not just for my sanity but for Patrick's too. Patrick was starting to feel alienated like I didn't want him, like he was replaceable. Replaceable Patrick was not. His resilience and determination are hands-down the best I've ever seen and what attracted me to him.

Eventually I'm going to have to have these conversations with Patrick. It was not going to go well. Maybe if I showered him with gifts, like my dad did to my mom it would be okay. Who was I fooling, I fucked up royally. I allowed one night of a fractured ego to destroy my once happy life and home.

I have a secret. A dirty, dark, horrible secret that no one would ever guess. The kind of secret that once you find out your life and the lives of those you love are forever changed. See, I am HIV positive and yes, I take meds whenever I care to remember. I haven't told anyone, not even my sexual partners, that, I am positive. Why? What's the point? Come on you know there are illnesses out there and still you want to engage in unprotected sex? That's your problem. You deserve whatever you get. I am the last person you would "assume" was positive. I am gorgeous and should have been someone's sugar baby. Conceited much? No, confident always. But no matter because alas, I am positive. It was all because I allowed myself to fall in love and trust someone. That shit won't happen again.

Right now, I am a bit of a community dick. I spread it wherever I can and if you are protected great, but if not oh well you roll the dice and hope you don't crap out. Horrible much? No, not really just hurt beyond measure and if I hurt why shouldn't others who take no concern not be hurt also. Condoms are always offered, and your answer should always be yes, but if the answer is no, then no one can expect me to care.

Whom am I to be concerned with their wellbeing if they are not concerned? I even act really concerned when they call me and tell me that I should get assessed because, they were positive. So stupid. Makes you just want to slap them on the forehead. You never know what's out here nowadays.

Life wasn't always so tragic (add dramatic flair here). No, seriously life was amazing but one fateful evening, one wrong decision led to multiple and here we are today. I mean it wasn't always horrible, at one time it was beautiful. Just like a fool, I was in love. Oh, to remember when, when life was simpler if ever being gay could be simple. That bitch Fernando. That was/is his name. I don't even know if he is still alive and frankly, I wouldn't even buy a fuck to care. He was an integral part of my past, which led to my present.

One would never imagine someone as beautiful as myself could be so ugly. It is what it is. Anyway, we were reliving the tragic steps it took for me to get to this point. Fernando. Tall, dark, and handsome, that is what I always called him. Sexy as all hell and delicious to boot. Met Fernando at a function with my cousin Stephanie. Stephanie was looking for a slide (easy pickup) and I was just out enjoying myself. Sightseeing the lay of the land and then he caught my eye. Mesmerizing he was. Just couldn't keep my eyes off of him and his smile was EVERYTHING!! Rows and rows of beautiful white teeth lined up just perfectly. When he came over and introduced himself as I was standing at the bar, I almost fainted. He smelled sooo good and his voice was deep and smooth. Smitten is the word that comes to mind but in hindsight I was in heat and lonely. Even someone such as I have a hard time finding quality individuals and not just trade (casual partner).

Everyone wants to be held at night and have a warm neck to snuggle into while being held in a tight embrace. Okay enough of skipping down memory lane that is definitely not the morale of the story. You are trying to figure out how I got so fucked up right? Well, you asked about it so here goes. Fernando and I had a world wind romance. After the first meeting, we were inseparable. He had me trying things I would have never tried. Started smoking weed, tried some Ecstasy, did a few threesomes. Anything he asked me for, I would try my hardest to accommodate. Talk about stupid and in love. Makes for a very dangerous concoction.

We had a wonderful time until it wasn't so wonderful. In the beginning we traveled to amazing places. All over the Caribbean and even went to Dubai. It was after Dubai that things turned horribly wrong. I will never forget that day. We ended up moving in together right before traveling because my lease was up, and it just made logical sense. A week after we returned, all of a sudden, I could not do anything right. I couldn't cook or even wash dishes right. If other people were around, he was amazing and then when they left it was as if a light switch was clicked on. Fernando turned into this other person. One that I didn't recognize, and I couldn't place. True Jekyll and Hyde.

He became abusive not physically because physically everyone would notice. As I said before I was hot, so I got a lot of stares. It was more like emotional and mental abuse and that's even harder to explain to people. You always get individuals saying, "Well why would you let him do that?" How do you explain affairs of the heart? The heart wants what the heart wants. It got really bad. He would criticize my clothing, my hair, even how I smelled if he didn't like my cologne. Fernando told me that I was worthless, that I was getting too fat to wear the clothes I wore and that he was the only one who would ever love me. It got to the point that my self-esteem just started going lower and lower and I started second-guessing myself.

Second-guessing who I was and what I could accomplish.

I was already going through after my mother and father died. It was hard navigating this life without my parents. It was especially hard being gay and navigating without support. My parents were the ones that got me through all the bullying and name calling I experienced. My parents were the ones that stopped me from getting depressed. It was my parents that would have warned me about Fernando and would have told me I deserved better. If they were still alive, I probably would not have gone down the road that I am currently traveling on. Okay that is another story for another day.

Any way back to that fucking asshole Fernando. I would come home every night and he would belittle me and make me feel less than. Chipping me away piece by piece. Found myself shrinking every time he entered a room. One thing Fernando would often do to humiliate me is being an inspector. He would do this by standing in the kitchen and watching me clean. Like he was supervising. Standing there leaned against the counter just watching while drinking a glass of water. Guess he needed to quench his thirst for all the demanding work HE was doing.

I know I could have just left but I wasn't sure if I was ready to leave. I still loved him and thought I would be able to change him. When he was nice, he made my entire day, but it never lasted. Like my mama used to say "Beware of an individual's representative. Once they are gone you have to deal with the real person. Always remember you can't change anyone who doesn't think they need to change. And you can't save anybody who doesn't want to be saved." No truer words have ever been spoken.

Even though things were bad there were times when we were good. There were times when he was sweet and nice. He would buy me wonderful things, he would take me out to nice dinners, he would treat me like he loved me, and I was important. Those times were minimal however they meant the world to me.

Miami. All roads ended in Miami. I'll never forget when he would take me to Miami. He would take me to parties, and we would have a great time. There were a few times when I believed that he slipped something in my drink. I couldn't prove it, but I would just be different. During those times I would become more promiscuous at these parties. I would go to the party and sleep with him and anybody else he brought over because I loved him or at least I thought I did. The last party was the worst by far. It was that party that I believed changed my entire life.

We had gone back to Miami to an all-white party. It was at this fancy mansion in South Beach. I still am not sure whose house it was, but it was fabulous. All I know is that I felt really important and that I was on Fernando's arm, and he was on mine. As a couple we were stunning, and I know we looked like superstars. For some reason this party was different. Felt different. First off, after we were there for only an hour, they locked the front doors. There was music playing and there were open areas where people were making out. As we were inspecting the house, we could see some people left bedroom doors open so you can see what they were doing. There were waiters walking around with whatever "candy" you wanted to partake in. I'm not talking about food either. There was Ecstasy, there was Molly, there was coke, whatever you wanted was right there for you. Yeah, this party felt different.

I got a drink and I just sat back and watched as people were just being openly promiscuous and not trying to hide it. I will admit that it was a bit of a turn on although it wasn't really my vibe as I was more private. At this particular moment I didn't know how deep I would end up going. Far deeper than I wanted to go. I wasn't partaking in any of the goodies being handed out and was just chilling. Fernando excused himself and then came back with a gummy. I have had edibles before, and they just made me more chilled. What I didn't know was this was not a normal edible. I continued drinking my drink and watching the activities. Call me stupid or naïve but I never thought Fernando would do anything to intentionally harm me. What I found out later is that was not true.

Fernando had spiked my drink without me knowing. All I remember is I had a gummy and a drink. Don't ask me what happened next. All I can recall is being in a room suddenly. I do remember being there being two other people in the room one was a girl and another a guy. Fernando came over and rubbed my face and told me to just behave and enjoy. Wasn't sure what that meant but I was feeling woozier. Later found out that the gummy was laced with fentanyl. I do remember that I didn't feel like myself and had no control over my body or mind. The guy started kissing me and the girl started rubbing on me and Fernando just sat and watched. I'll admit it felt good although wasn't really in the girls, but it felt good. She started to kiss me and the next thing I knew was we were all naked. I found out that the girl was actually trans, so her boobs came with extra beneath her waist. It was enjoyable for a minute and then it started feeling brutal. It became very animalistic. I was being choked by somebody's penis in my mouth somebody was fucking me. I just didn't know what was going on I was out of my mind, and he just sat there with a smile and smirk on his face. He just sat and watched and did nothing even when I begged him to stop it. After it was all done, he apologized profusely as I laid in a ball on the bed. I felt dirty and was disgusted with him and myself. Again, I forgave him because I was in love. Love is bullshit.

A few weeks after the trip to Miami, I started not feeling so good. I had a cold and no matter what I did it would not go away. Started even missing days at work. Eventually my manager saw me and told me maybe I should go to the doctor. I went and it was the worst diagnosis I could have ever been told. At the doctor's office they did a full work up including taking blood. It was then that I was told that I was HIV positive. Fernando was the only one I had with unprotected except for the Miami trip where no one was protected. I was devastated.

I cried just a little, but I was enraged. Went home and I proceeded to throw shit at Fernando. Plates, cups, forks, spoons, lamps, whatever I could grab, I tossed towards his head. Proceeded to go out and use a pipe on his car. It was then that he punked out and called the cops on me. The man I loved call the cops on me. Spent two days in the police station with a bunch of cretins. It was at that moment that I realized my life was over and love was pure bullshit. After I was released, I had the cops come with me as I packed my stuff in my suitcase. After that I walked away. Fernando was there looking remorseful however I know that was a façade. After I left, I totally blocked him. I slept at Stephanie's, but I couldn't stay there because

Duane and his son came every couple of weeks, so it was too crowded. Eventually found me a new place.

Fernando came to my job a few times. I told his ass never to come to my place of employment or call me fucking again. He tried for a while, but I was done. Love taught me to proceed with caution with all men. I decided to just fuck around. If you had protection, then you were safe, you won the prize. If you chose the no protection way, you just rolled the dice. Everybody knows that you eventually will crap out when you roll dice. Wished I cared but I didn't. My life is hell now. No parents, no support system and HIV hanging over my head. I just fucked whoever I wanted and had no intention of falling in love again. Yeah, beauty is overrated, and love is definitely overrated.

Why should I give a fuck?

Why should I care for anyone?

Nobody really cared about me. It is entirely up to you if you decide to mess with me. Every day we make choices, and it is a choice if you want to play with protection. If not, you end up playing Russian Roulette with your life.

I am as gorgeous as I am deadly literally.

I am the perfect definition that looks can kill.

Justin

Okay, time to put on my game face. Always had to put on airs when I walked into this place. It helped to have Crystal on my arm. More on her a little later. Anyway, the business was all my sorry father ever gave me. He took more than he gave. His sorry ass took the most important thing to me when he took my mother away. It was the main reason I was uninterested in falling in love.

Love sucks.

Fuck love.

It was because my mother was so in love with that asshole called my father, that she continued to forgive him.

Deadbeat left when I was seven and came back when I was ten. From my eavesdropping skills, I learned he left to be with another woman. And yet, mom still took him back. She said life was easier when he was around. That we didn't struggle as much when he was there. Truthfully, I loved it when it was just mom and me. There was no drama and no arguing or fighting. Well, one day the asshole left for a few days with no explanation. My mom was so distraught she rented a car to follow him from work to see where he was going. She cared way too much. Kind of wish she cared about me as much. I'm not sure what happened next, all I know is that the police and a social worker were at the door telling me that my parents died in a fiery crash. That bastard took her from me. I fucking hated him.

Anyway, I was able to stay in the house we had. Maybe it was the lie I told them that my grandmother would be checking in on me. Little did they know that the lady they met was my neighbor and not my grandmother. I slipped her some money to help me out. By the time I turned eighteen I had inherited the house and the company my father owned. I sold the house but kept the company. Felt good to have my dad's pride and joy under my control. Real good.

I walked into the factory and greeted everyone. I saw Matt. "Hey Matt, how's it going? How's your boyfriend? I mean your husband?" I asked and flicked my wrist down in a derogatory way. Matt just shook his head and said fine and walked away. That made me chuckle. I could not understand how Matt could be gay. How could someone be in a gay relationship, any single relationship for that matter? It was all so boring. Especially when there is so much dick and pussy readily available. Shit, I know I am fine. I have clean cut hair, with a chiseled face and a body that was beyond physically fit. The gym was my second home. I had no shortage of male or female suitors.

Crystal, who was my current "girlfriend" was hot too. She had tits and ass for days and she shared a peculiar appetite like I did. I gave Matt such a hard time because I could tell Matt was well endowed below the waist. Just the thought excited me. I often envisioned what being with Matt would actually be like. Yeah, Yeah, I know I have a girlfriend. She was actually more like my mustache instead of a beard. I'm not gay although others would beg to differ. I am bisexual which is not gay. I loved the softness of a woman and thoroughly enjoyed the hardness of a man. See I was a switch. I was both a dom and a sub. With women I was dominate, I loved being in control. With men I was more of a sub or a bottom.

There is something about a nice size penis stretching my mouth to its limits that does something for me. And to feel balls slapping my ass while someone is pounding me, that feeling is amazing. Crystal loved to watch. Think she enjoys seeing me getting punked out. She said there was something sexy about watching me have sex with another man. That is what I like about her, her open mind and sense of adventure. It also helped that she was bisexual too. I was fine with it and had no interest in watching. We just gave each other space to be ourselves. No labels or attachments.

That's why I don't understand why Matt is with Patrick. Matt is divine. I could just feel him in my mouth until my jaws hurt. Stop it, Stop it, you are at work. But if I was the slight bit honest, I got a little moist every time I thought about Matt. Oh no, no, no. One should never shit where they eat.

Anyway, to me, bisexual sounded so much sexier than gay. Plus having a girlfriend thwarted all the questions anyone might have. I have had people ask me why I don't try a transexual woman since it was the best of both worlds. I tried it once, something about chicks with dicks didn't do it for me. I wanted titties with pussy and my balls with pecs.

Yes, I said that motherfucking shit.

Drop the damn mic.

Don't get me wrong, I have friends that are trans, and they are quite gorgeous and handsome depending on whom you are looking at. It is just hard to explain for me. I have no preference over a woman or a man, it's just how I wake up in the morning what I feel for.

Until I met Crystal. I met a lot of women who would say the most derogatory things to me when they found out I liked men too. I've been called everything short of a child of God. Wow, I haven't thought about God in quite some time. Especially since he let that bastard take my mom away from me. What type of almighty wonderful God would do that to a child, to a woman who praised you so much.

I actually have been thinking about my mom a lot lately. Let me get to my office so I could really think about this without being analyzed by the staff. Crystal won't pay me much mind since she stays on her damn phone taking pictures most of the time. I close my door and sit behind my amazing glass desk. I changed all the furniture as soon as I inherited the company. I refused to live in the past and sat at the desk my father sat at. He might have built this company, but I came in and made it all mine. He is lucky I even buried his ass. I was going to have him unclaimed however his cousins guilted me and his other children, (yes, his ass had four other kids with four other women) wanted him buried. Since I got the business and the house, I was nice enough to give them something from his insurance policy.

Not their fault he was a limp dickhead. Plus, my mom left me with a nice amount of money to survive on so besides the business, I needed nothing from him. Crystal said something the other day that got me thinking of my mom. When I asked her randomly how she felt about me being bisexual she said, "if you like it, I love it." My mom used to say that all the time.

Why did love tend to leave so many causalities in its wake?

What purpose did it actually serve?

Being that I liked having my cake and eating it too, could I fall in love with one person?

Do I even want to?

Being a bisexual man is so hard. Everyone calling you gay when you are not. Women despising you because you like men, men despising you because you like women, no one understanding who I really am.

I am a lot more complex than my sexual appetites. I have a myriad of haunting dreams and unrealized realities. Yes, I loved to be dominated every now and again and have a man yank me by my neck. I also liked to run my hands down a woman's back right at the curvature of where her waist and ass connect.

My lips loved the taste of pussy and the creaminess of sperm in my throat.

Could I explain it? Nope.

Did I want to? Nope.

I just want what I want and what I don't ever want is love ruining the carnal nature of my lust and desires. Plus, what has loved ever done for me but bring headache and pain.

CHAPTER FIVE - THE PERPLEXED ONE

Diane

I was sitting on the window seat in our room looking at him or her or whatever it is he calls himself these days get ready for work. Tamia's "Stranger in my House" was playing repeat in my head and has been for the past few weeks. Twenty-five years together and who the hell is this person? The person who told me a few weeks ago that their life was a lie. A sham. That the man I loved was not really a man at all. No that wasn't fair. No need to bash what you can't understand. But that was just it, I didn't understand. I just couldn't. How could I understand how Rob had suddenly decided Roberta was who he now wanted to be? Twenty-five years, twenty-five fucking years of my life!!! I had spent all that time loving this man.

Giving my body to this man. Birthing this man's children. Building a life and a home with this man here. This man who informed me that he would prefer to no longer be a man. He would prefer to be a woman. Maybe it was my fault. Maybe I chose the wrong man. Maybe in an effort not to be lonely I married a man who could never love me in the matter in which I deserved or needed. If I am honest with myself there were signs. Signs in which I readily ignored because he said he loved me. I mean yeah, he could have been more passionate, more affectionate but I just thought that was just his upbringing. No, this shit wasn't my fault. This was Rob's fault. He lied. He lied to himself, and he lied to me. He knew for years that he wasn't happy, and he strung me along and kept it all a secret until he got fucking caught. I will never forget that day as long as I live.

I was supposed to be at work but hadn't been feeling well all morning. Rob gave me his perfunctory kiss on my forehead before he left for work that morning and proceeded to ask me if I was going to the office. I said yes, I have a deadline to complete so I needed to go in. We are semi empty nesters with both kids in college out of state. Rob Jr. in California and Jessica in Seattle, both tired of the crazy east coast weather. Rob said, "Okay well I'll see you tonight." He put on his gray scarf and cashmere coat and left. I struggled to get dressed and drove to the train station to commute to the office. I was at work for only three hours before Barbara my boss came in and said "Diane, you don't look so good. Maybe you should go home and get some rest." "But the deadline?" I said in return. "What good is a deadline if you can't deliver the pitch? Go home, get some rest, and come back after the weekend. By then you should be refreshed and renewed. I need you next week on top of your game." So, I agreed and packed up my bag and caught the next train home.

I ended up taking a cab home because I was not up to driving myself home. I remember thinking, Rob can just drive me back to the station tonight to get my car. That one action started the avalanche of discovery.

Because I didn't drive home, I didn't see Rob's car in the garage. Because I did not come through the garage was also why Rob didn't know I came home early. See the garage door has a chime on it to let anyone in the house know someone was coming through the garage. Instead, I went through the front door. Which should have been a heads up because the alarm was disarmed, and I ALWAYS put on the alarm. Remember I was sick and all I wanted to do was get back in bed, so the alarm was not in the forefront of my mind. I remember I dropped my things by the door, took off my shoes and went upstairs to our room. Only to find my husband of twenty-five years with his back turned to me, tucking his penis between his legs. I quickly moved out of eyesight to watch as he put on a device, that I later found out was called a gaff to assist with tucking. Rob then proceeded to put on some panties, pantyhose and then some heels. After seeing this I began to feel sicker than when I came home. Then Rob turned around and I saw his face. His face was fully made up with makeup. I couldn't contain my gasp. Rob looked up so fast and can you believe that he had the audacity of covering up his chest like he had breasts. I chuckled at him. Right now, it is funny but then it made me nauseous. Not because a man was dressing as a woman. It was because it was my man who was doing it.

Who was this person and what the hell is going on? I grasped the door ledge to hold myself up so I wouldn't fall, took a deep breath, and said as calmly as possible "Rob what in the entire fuck is going on?" Rob started stuttering some nonsense that made no sense until I put up my hand and politely walked away and went downstairs to the living room. Went and grabbed my chenille blanket that was on the couch, laid across the chaise and closed my eyes. I did not have the energy or will to deal with any of this. I drifted off to sleep and when I woke up the clock said five. I was not sure if it was morning or evening. It was dark both times this time of year, so it wasn't clear. I got up and stretched and went upstairs to our bedroom. Rob was on the bed sleeping looking like plain old regular Rob. Sleeping so peaceful and looking so handsome. Maybe I dreamed up the whole thing. No, my imagination was not that good.

I went to Rob and shook him until he woke up. "We need to talk.!" Rob woke up all startled and wide eyed. "What, what's going on Diane? Why are you shaking me like a raving lunatic?" "I just need to understand what the hell is actually going on with you?" "What do you mean?" Rob said sitting up on one elbow. "Really Rob? Really? Do I look like a brand-new fool? This is what we are going to do? Okay, then explain to me why I came home sick to find my husband in drag.

Are you a drag queen?

Are you gay?

What the hell is going on because hell I just don't understand? What do I tell the kids?"

"I'm mm, I'm mm sorry. I'm not gay at least I don't think I am. I am transgender." Rob said. "What the hell does that even mean Rob?" I asked. "It means I feel like a woman inside not a man." Rob started with his hands on his head. "What does that mean, we have sex, we have kids!!

What about our life?

What about our friends?

What about our church?

Wha, What about me?"

What happens now?"

I rattled quickly. "Diane, I don't know, I just don't know how to explain it all. I just know that I have never felt like a man." Rob stuttered. "I felt like something was different, off. It has nothing to do with you and the kids. I have always felt this way. As long as I can remember." Rob proceeded to tell me. It was all too much. "Rob, you have to leave for a few days so I can gather myself. I don't just know what to make out of all of this." I told him. I then turned and walked away. I didn't know what I was going to do.

My entire married life was a lie.

Now what? What do I do next?

How do I explain what I don't understand?

CHAPTER SIX - THE RELIEVED ONE

Robert

Last night was full of emotions. It definitely was devastating. Not sure if I felt more sad or relieved about last night. I know I felt ashamed. Not ashamed about who I was but ashamed that Diane had to find out this way. She was supposed to be at work. I had this big elaborate plan on how to tell her. How to explain how I felt inside. It was a big mess now. Above all else, as messed up as it is, I felt really happy it was finally out. I mean I was upset that I hurt Diane. Didn't want her to find out this way. Truthfully was trying to find a way to tell her but just never had the courage to. The tension in our house at the moment was thick as a heavy fog. I hate to keep saying this, but it was relieving because I finally felt free. Free to finally live my truth. I felt truly seen, now I could live out loud and am so happy not to hide anymore.

All my life all I did was hide. Became what everyone wanted me to be. All my life I felt unseen. Like I was a joke, and I didn't get the punchline. I tried hard, really, really hard. Look, I played basketball in college, met Diane, married Diane and we have two children, RJ and Jessica. Brought the house, the cars, damn at one point we even had a dog. Checked all the boxes and had everyone fooled except myself. Never once in my life did, I feel like a man. I have always felt like there was a mistake that I was born male. Like I got on the wrong line when they were handing out genders. You know girls on the left, boys on the right and I went right in error because I momentarily forgot my directions. Always felt like I was wearing the wrong skin. There was longing in my soul, longing to be a woman but never could I voice this out loud because how could I make someone understand what I just now to begin to understand. Always having to consciously watch my mannerisms so not to be teased like my cousin Antoine.

He was teased horribly, especially by his dad and our uncle. I didn't see Antoine much then and only when we went to church now. He is the choir director. Tried to get Diane to change churches and she politely told me she was not giving up her church for anyone. When we were younger, I was not allowed to be around Antoine because they said he was trouble. Never told what kind of trouble although the rumor mills buzzed about prostitution or enticing married men. People always had a lot to say, and I was disinterested in engaging them. As I was growing up, I learned how to hide when I put on my makeup. Even tried hard to actively try to enjoy sex with Diane. Let me clarify sex wasn't bad it just did not feel natural. It often felt forced. I had an unwanted body part that dangled between my legs. Haven't had sex lately in a while. I had poor Diane suggesting I consider Viagra. Sex with Diane felt hard when all I wanted was softness. There were times I wished I could be soft like Diane is. Honestly, I think I've gotten tired of fighting how I was feeling inside. I didn't care about the 25 years married, didn't care as selfish as it sounds about the kids either. Just cared how I've always felt inside, and I never, never felt whole. I was heading into possibly the second half of my life and tired of living for everyone else but myself. All of this time my body felt like I had on a costume. A costume that didn't fit right. Don't get me wrong, we have had a dream life. White picket fence, two kids, great careers, great community. Everything was great, great, great, I felt like an actor in a grand play. None of them fit. It wasn't who I was born to be. I am trapped in a fantasy I never wanted to take part in. How do you explain that, that you feel different? 25 years, no scratch that for 47 years I pretended to be someone I wasn't.

The great pretender finally got caught. The jig was up. The way I was caught yesterday was just plain embarrassing. I was a little too grown to be caught in an elaborate game of dress up. I only took off because again Diane was supposed to be at work. Worst possible scenario ever.

Fuck!!!

How come the garage door didn't make noise or the kitchen alarm didn't sound?

Damn, damn, damn, damn!!!!!

Diane and I have to sit down and have a rational discussion. Not a screaming match, a real heart to heart.

What do we tell the kids, our friends, our neighbors?

When do we tell all of them?

What do we tell our church?

What is happening between Diane and I now?

What is my next move? Should I tell her now that I started taking the female hormones. Do I tell her where I am really going when I play golf? Or those boy trips out of town. The ones when I am actually in another state walking around like a woman. I almost got busted once in Chicago, which was a really close call.

I did all the "manly" things as my dad would have said. I was considered an all-American boy whose now a man. Played football for over ten years. I am an usher at our church. When was it going to be my time to live my truth? I am tired of hiding. I needed to figure out what's next, especially with Diane and me.

Diane came up here really pissed off today wanted to know if our sex was real and was I he, she, or they? What were my new pronouns?

Hell, I didn't even know this was all new to me too. She asked if I was a drag queen and I tried to explain to her that I was trans. That I wanted my pronouns to be she and her and Diane was confused. Diane wanted to know if she was now bisexual or a lesbian if I was now a woman.

How do you explain to somebody special, somebody that you loved for so long that you want to be someone else? Yeah, this was going to be a long difficult conversation.

I had to prepare myself because I didn't know what to do.

Xiomara

"Stop it, just stop it!"

Damn Xiomara, get it the fuck together. That's what kept saying to myself as I sat on the damn bathroom floor. You couldn't make this shit up. Who has these kinds of problems? And who could I speak to when I kept her a secret. The secret that broke my fucking heart. No, she tore my heart clear out of my chest.

WHAT THE HELL!!!

What was supposed to be a romantic weekend turned into a clear shit show. I was ready, finally ready to give it all up. To claim her and make her mine. To fight for her and to take whatever came with doing that. Amanda had been patient. Way too patient, with all the bullshit I had put her through. It was her patience that I loved most about her. Ten years and now what the hell am I supposed to do? What I must definitely do is get off this damn bathroom floor and get myself together before Duane brings DJ back home. I do not have the patience nor fortitude to explain to my 5-year-old son or his damn nosey ass father why I was upset.

Hell, I am not upset, I am devastated. Fully and completely devastated. Amanda walked into the apartment as my girlfriend and left as my ex. I haven't slept since she left two days ago and every time, I come to the bathroom I start sobbing like a baby. The bathtub was still full of dissolved bubbles just sitting there sad on top of the water. I didn't even have the energy to empty the tub. I felt like the sad suds that I am currently looking at. It's as if someone just punched me right in the center of my chest. I just keep playing in my mind how she said she can't and won't do this anymore. I'm so confused. Practically begged her not to go and bombarded her with a bunch of questions.

Who was she leaving me for?

What could I do to make her stay?

When did she make the decision that I wasn't what she wanted anymore?

Why was she leaving me?

How could she leave after all this time, especially when I was ready to be all hers?

I did everything for her no matter what she asked whenever I could. She just walked out of the door and out of my life. Girl, get it together. Blow your nose, wash your face, and clean up all this mess. Pick up the candles and pick up all these damn rose petals on the floor. All the effort for nothing, no not for nothing. Just a sad reminder of all that was.

Amanda has been ghosting me and hasn't answered any of the over 20 voicemails or any of the text messages I left her. I can't even leave her anymore messages because it says her voicemail is full and when I send her text messages, they go to green which means she has shut her phone off. What in the entire fuck?

I mean I admit I did my share of shit to Amanda, but she said she forgave me. She asked me to go with her six years ago to Arizona for a year. Amanda had to go there for work and wanted me to go with her. I kept telling her I wasn't ready to let anyone know about us yet and wasn't sure how one would explain leaving the state to move with her "best friend" for work. That's what I told my family that she was just my best friend. It helped to alleviate any undue questions. When we were lying next to one another I told her I liked the fact that no one knew about us. That made life easier for us. With no one knowing the intricacies of our relationship, we had to solve all problems by ourselves. No outside thoughts or opinions. Just us. The problem with a secret is you couldn't tell anyone how you felt. How happy you were and how you found love that was pure. I was already going through withdrawals, and it has only been two days.

Amanda stayed constantly on my mind. The more she gave me, the more I wanted. I didn't deserve or even had a right to want more, however, there I always was. My chest still hurts. Wasn't sure if was because I had been crying nonstop for twenty-four hours or if it was because I was heartbroken. Can't people die of heartbreak?

If I die, could Duane even take care of DJ?

Can't die of a heartbreak nobody knew about. I just can't lose her. She was a magnet, and I was nickel. No matter how hard I tried I couldn't pull away from her. It was like we were kismet beings, not only metaphorically but literally also. I didn't want to keep her a secret. I wanted to scream on the rooftops about how happy I was and how very happy she made me. How could I do that when I couldn't tell my mom and definitely couldn't tell my abuela when she was alive. My abuela was dead set against lesbian relationships. She couldn't understand how two women could build a family and build a relationship. Marriage was for procreating not for pleasure. I could never explain to anyone our connection.

It was surreal how I felt about her. There was a draw like a moth to a flame, no matter how hard I tried to pull away. The problem is that I didn't want to pull away, I wanted to draw nearer. I always wanted to be in her presence and now it feels like there is a hole in the center of my soul.

Why did she leave me?

Was I not good enough for her?

I have had other women just none of them compared to Amanda. Amanda was the Ying to my Yang. She saw all the good and bad parts of me. All I needed her to do was to be patient. Why couldn't she be patient?

All I needed for her was to be a little more patience.

Was I not worth waiting for?

Besides DJ she was the best part of me.

How can I feel complete when pieces of me are now missing?

How did I love her and hate her for destroying my life all at the same time?

CHAPTER EIGHT - THE CLANDESTINE ONE

Amanda

Xiomara is probably freaking out right now. She has sent me a million text messages since I left last night. I had to put my phone on do not disturb to stop from stressing. I can honestly say that last night was the worst night of my life. I mean it started off beautifully with our hello kiss. The softness of her was simply amazing. The feel of her body. To never be able to touch her again. Sweet Xiomara. Yeah, she was so sweet. Her kisses, her hugs, damn even her pussy was sweet like mangoes and oh so succulent. I will definitely miss her, but I had to choose me.

If I knew Xiomara, and I knew Xiomara, she would be sitting there questioning everything. She is constantly asking five w's and an h. She asked when I walked out the door. Who was I leaving her for? The real answer is for me. I found I was giving her more and receiving nothing, but amazing sex and sex is never enough. Then of course the What came next. What happened to make me leave? Hell, what didn't happen? Based on our history there was never a moment where we could just be us.

First of all, Xiomara was all the way in the closet like back in the closet with the dust. Xiomara's family had no idea that she loved women. They were super conservative and believed that a woman should be with a man. How antiquated of a belief system. I had to deal with that all of this time and because I loved her, I supported her guise. Oh, and let's not forget about her getting pregnant by a dude from her old neighborhood one night while she was drunk. I personally swear he is gay or bisexual if he slept with Xiomara. Apparently, she got pregnant when we were on break. The only thing is:

WE WERE NEVER ON BREAK!!

I had to move across country for my job for one year. Even asked her to go with me but of course she could not or would not go because she could not leave her family. Plus, how could she explain to her family why she was moving away to stay with her "best friend". This is what her family thought we were. I was honestly okay that she was bisexual although I was not. I was what they called a gold star lesbian, I have never been with a man and did not desire to be with one. Just wasn't my thing. If I am being honest, it did hurt that I was a secret. Everyone should know about our love, however Xiomara had so much to lose so a secret I remained. Duane Jr. was also who I would miss. I truly loved DJ, her son so very much.

That was my buddy. I'm going to miss the little dude terribly. There was nothing my Xiomara could do to make me stay. She has no idea how long it took for me to make the decision to leave. This wasn't an easy decision for me at all. I deserve more than being a secret. Being her secret was no more than being a temporary fix for her. She said she loves me, but I've watched her over and over again make mistakes when it came to men. It is always when she was disappointed, I was there to lift her back up and show her love. It was exhausting and I was tired. She then asked, "Why was I leaving and how could I leave her now?" I just couldn't do this anymore.

I made myself a promise after Tianna that I would never be a secret again and yet here I was yet again. Tianna was my first real "relationship" ever. I have known I loved women since I was five years old. Loved the way they moved, the way they smelled, the taste of their skin but mainly their overall softness. My first kiss was even with a girl when I was ten years old. To this day I still remember the smell of her bubblegum lip gloss and how very soft her lips were against mine. I never had an attraction to the opposite sex. Nothing about men intrigued me enough to want to have sex with them. Strong feminine sexy women intrigued me. I was feminine and fly so my lady most definitely had to be the same. As I said Tianna was my first. You never forget your first.

Tianna was amazing, simply amazing. I met her by accident. I was supposed to be meeting a friend and went to the wrong address. I walk in and this stunning woman stood there. I asked for directions, and it was her laugh and the look in her eyes that snatched my soul clear out of my body. After exchanging pleasantries, it was Tianna that asked for my number. We exchanged numbers and I went on my merry way and thought nothing of it, that was until she called.

Our first experience was awkward yet unbelievable. I would not change anything about it. Never thought I would love a woman that much. Tianna was incredibly juicy and the longer we were together, the more I wanted to learn how to make her wetter and juicer. Remembering her is making me lick my lips because it was that good. She turned me all the way out and she showed me things I didn't think I would ever do or could even do. She had me open and I was here for all of it. Even when Tianna met Jonathan, we were still strong. Even when she and Jonathan got engaged, we were still seeing one another. Everyone thought I was one of her closest friends and had no idea that we were more.

In all honesty I would've stayed for Tianna had our last situation not turned out the way it did. One day we were going super-hot and heavy at her apartment that she shared. If you remember Tianna had a fiancé named Jonathan and they moved in before the wedding. We had been going at it for two hours and it was just so good, and she tasted amazing. I had no intention of stopping and we were so into it that we never heard the key in the door. We were so into each other that we couldn't even stop scramble or try to make an excuse of why my head was in the pussy of my "close friend". There was no way to explain why my face was all shiny and sticky. No way to explain the smell of pussy that was heavily permeating the air. Tianna did a lot of scrambling and trying to explain. I didn't because the truth is I wasn't sorry if I could, I would do it again. He just happened to be added to a situation that was already occurring.

I loved Tianna way more than Jonathan ever could and how could I make excuses that his fiancé was on my breath. He would smell it every time I opened my mouth to explain. Hell, as I said before I planned on keeping her even after she married him because it was just too hard to let her go. Unfortunately, though in that situation, I was the third wheel.

The only two women I have ever been with Tiana and Xiomara. Both told everyone that I was their best friend, and I was knee-deep in each of their pussies. Yeah, I am not really sure how we would equate the word "friend" to these situations. Tiana is a sweet memory and feels like Xiomara might be another one eventually. I love Xiomara so very much, I just couldn't take the life, the uncertainty, and the unwillingness to admit that you just love who you love. It shouldn't matter what gender they are. I loved both of them and Tiana broke my heart because of course she chose Jonathan. Xiomara broke my heart because she didn't choose me. Yeah, I would always come second fiddle as long as I was a secret. We both deserved better. I just know that Xiomara needs to figure out what she wants to do for herself.

I deserve somebody who wants to love me and love me just the way I am. Unfortunately, Xiomara could not do that. Her family didn't even know she was bisexual. I am going to miss her horribly though.

Ever since I met her, she was just...different. We met at work originally, but I don't shit where I eat so I refused to mess with her. She actually pursued me relentlessly, but I told her we can only be friends since we worked together. That lasted a few years until I found a new job. After that all bets were off. Our first date was Starbucks just to talk. We shut down Starbucks. We sat for five hours joking and laughing and enjoying each other's company. It was a great time. We finally exchanged numbers and I thought I would never hear from her again. It was two years since I left, maybe she had found someone else. And then she called. The sound of her voice over the phone was so enticing. It was rich, full and you could practically feel a vibration in every word she spoke. Maybe it was just me but something about her voice did it for me and made me want her to keep doing it over and over again. We eventually started out scorching hot and would make love for hours. I loved it when we kissed. Our lips just matched, and her kisses were so soft. Actually, I loved all the softness of her. Her body felt amazing against my fingers. Loved how it felt to touch her breasts, to lick her nipples and how they felt in my mouth. How wonderful, so wonderful to watch her face contort as I made her cum. I loved Xiomara because she sees my flaws, she sees my heart and my pain. She loves my quirkiness and I love her sooo very much. I just can't keep being in the shadows, being the secret.

Even though she was all I ever wanted as long as I was the "best friend" it would never be enough. Breaking up with her was the only thing I was left to do. By far that was the hardest thing I've ever done. Maybe me letting her go will help her figure out who she really was, so she could hopefully figure it out. If that meant I have to leave pieces of my heart with her I will. I am not sure how that will work because even as I sit here and try not to think about her, I want her.

I still want her really badly.

Duane "Deliciousness"

Tired of being stuck.

Riding the bus from my downtown home was my peace. It allowed me to think and ponder about where my life was headed. Right now, I feel stuck. I made a hell of mistakes but like my grandmother always said "Life is like a pencil. There is an eraser because we make mistakes." I loved my grandmother; she was my lifeline and helped me get through some of the worst parts of my life. I lived with her, and she kept me level. My parents were wherever. They were dope fiends looking for their next fix. They left me on a bench outside my grandmother's building when I was seven and took off. Those assholes didn't even have the decency to take me up to her apartment. If it had not been for one of the neighbors God only knows what would have occurred.

I still lived mostly with my grandmother. All I could do was sigh. Yeah, I am stuck still staying at home but dwelling in the past won't fix anything at this moment. Plus, people watching was so exhilarating. People always thought they were hiding their emotions well, but if you looked at them you could see their stories on their faces. I loved sitting in the window seat by myself. Really and truly hated it when I had to sit in a two-seater and had some random person sat next to me. Being so close to someone that wasn't invited in my space was annoying as hell. Today was a lucky day, the bus was pretty empty.

There was a lot to unpack in my head before I got home uptown. I must admit the highlight of my day was seeing Mark come into the restaurant where I worked and nearly choke on his ribeye when I placed the spinach on his table. I can only assume the woman who was trying way too hard was his wife. She had put on too much makeup, and I saw the Birkin bag she must carry hanging off her chair. Plus, the big rock on her left hand was a clear sign. I politely asked Mark "Sir are you okay? Maybe you should drink some water." Gave my megawatt smile and turned away.

I started laughing and gave a bit of a chuckle. Wonder if she knew just 24 hours previously her man's legs were in the air, and he was begging me to go harder and deeper. I'm always amused when I see one of them frequent the restaurant. Them being the down low curious men that come up to me frequently while I am working. One of them even gave me the name Deliciousness because he said everything about me was delicious, huh delicious. That was an amazing way to have someone describe you. Delicious.

No one would ever assume I was gay, although there was no look called "gay". I was very discreet with myself because I did not want all the questions and labels. Even made Stephanie my beard so my rouse was intact. It is a golden rule for me to keep my body tight and right. My hair is always freshly cut, and my lines were always sharp. Women hit on me all the time but that is not my particular flavor of ice cream. I mean women are beautiful creatures, I love watching them, and love their strength, just have no desire for them.

Living in the hood it was not easy to appear soft. It was because of that that I stayed so tough and hard. If niggas smelled a hint of weakness, they pounce on it. One instance I remember was when I planned on coming out to my grandma and I was heading home. Pure chaos was happening when I approached the building. There was a bunch of yelling and clothes being thrown out the window and poor David.

David was running around trying to grab all his stuff because the crackheads were lurking to see what they could grab. Of course, everyone was standing around looking and cracking jokes, but no one was helping. I stepped up and helped him out and even ran upstairs and gave him an old bag so he could put his stuff in. His father was yelling something out the window in Hindu, but I didn't understand. Mr. Singh owned the bodega around the corner so the whole neighborhood knew him. The whole neighborhood also knew that David was gay and every day the neighborhood cretins found a way to point that out. I always felt bad for David and was always nice to him. It was sad that people still didn't accept gay people. They were still people, just loved outside of what others called "normal". The situation with David made me realize that coming out was not going to happen as long as I lived in the projects.

There were some that suspected until I had my son DJ. DJ was not planned and no I was not in a relationship with a woman when I had him. That is an entire other debacle, Xiomara. She was a piece of work to say the least. I hated getting off the bus at my stop. I was like the Jay-Z song "raised in the projects with roaches and rats." There was so much I hated. Hated the broken glass pieces I had to pick out of the treads of my Timberlands. One time there was a crack vial stuck in the treads. Hated holding my breath in the elevator because it smelled like piss. Apparently, it was too hard to go to your apartment and go to the bathroom. Absolutely hated the dead eyes of the majority of my neighbors. They looked lost and beaten. Like they have given up and just settled this was their life. I wanted more for myself, more for DJ.

DJ. Who would have thought I would be so in love with such a little being. DJ originally was a massive mistake. DJ's mother Xiomara was an old high school friend. We became instant friends in high school, especially because both of us were loners and didn't hang out with a bunch of people. Didn't know what happened to her after high school and then I saw her in the neighborhood bar. She was sitting alone drinking and I recognized her and said it was stupid to sit alone when we could sit together. She laughed but looked sad. Said her and her boyfriend were on a break because he had to go across country for his job.

We proceeded to drink for hours and next thing I know we were in her apartment and making out. Xiomara had amazing kisses and as drunk as I was my perception could be skewed. All I know is I woke up the next day in her nice apartment horrified. As a consolation she was also horrified. We scrambled our good-byes and I know I put it in a do not open file in my mind. Being considered bisexual was not a label I ever wanted to carry.

And then she called me six months later to tell me she was pregnant, and it was mine. I called her a lie. I told her there was no way I was the father off of one time together and I think we used protection (remember we were all the way twisted). Xiomara asked me to meet her later that evening after work. So, I went to the house and there she stood belly and all, looking exquisite with the biggest frown on her face. So, we sat down, and we talked about why I thought I wasn't the father, and she dropped the biggest bombshell on me. She was the same as me, all the way undercover. I would never have guessed, and I guess neither would she.

We shared our experiences on why we were uncover and the burden it held. So, we ended up having DJ and he was everything to me. My life was never easy, but it was manageable. I hated bringing DJ to the projects. I didn't want him to think that this was life. Being around crackheads was not normal. It was where I grew up and I wanted better for my son. Stephanie was my other heart because she accepted me for me. She didn't judge my situations and my promiscuity.

All she asked was that I stay safe. I was safe most of the time. Only that one time I fell in love with Frank, the one who nicknamed me Deliciousness. Rule number one: Never let the heart get involved. These were flings. Just fun times with undercover men. I loved the lack of commitment with these men and the gifts and money helped also. Heh, I was the undercover sugar baby, LOL. These men were such a blast. Frank was different, he cared. He was concerned with my life and my wellbeing. He asked about my son and provided anything he needed. Frank was the reason I wanted to come out. That was until I saw what happened to David and I realized it would be too risky. Frank was willing to leave his wife for me. But I just couldn't do it and for Frank that was the deal breaker. After that it became a game. Who could I screw and walk away? I was sad I had to live in the closet but what would coming out do for me? Would it make my life in the projects easier? Would it help me get out of there quicker? Dealing with the down low guys was the safest. I kept their secret, and they kept mine. Their wives were their problems, not mine. My only problem and concern are making sure that DJ is okay. I would do whatever it was to give him a better life.

It was definitely a lonely life and sometimes made me incredibly. The bed was lonely at night. All I wanted was to cuddle and sleep up under someone all night. Someone to help me keep warm.

In the meantime, I will just buy some more blankets and live in the what ifs.

CHAPTER TEN - THE SECRETIVE ONE

Bria

I am going straight to hell.

Straight no chaser, don't pass go, just know I am going to hell.

Especially after the things I let Stephanie do to me last night. It was so disgusting, but it felt oh so very good. I was so ashamed of myself I couldn't even look her in the eye afterwards and when I did, I couldn't stop blushing. It was so sexy, so sensual, just so, so, um. Who would have thought there were so many routes to pleasure?

"Yes, ma'am, I will focus." My mom was yelling at me that I wasn't focused, and the truth was I wasn't. I could still taste her in my mouth. I can still smell her on my skin. As I licked my swollen lips I tried to smile, and my heart jumped. I am trying not to smile so hard because then my mom would start with the Jeopardy questions. My nipples were still sore, and it hurt to walk.

Yeah, I'm going to hell.

Being here in church and thinking these blasphemous thoughts. I couldn't stop thinking about them though. Every time she crossed my mind I felt a jolt between my legs, and I got a little moist. There wasn't a part of me she didn't lick. She licked me like I was an ice cream cone from head to toe.

Damn. Love.

An amazing and scary feeling.

Love followed no rules or parameters.

Love was just love. One couldn't help who they loved because love followed no rhyme or reason. Our love was abstruse. There was no explanation on the how or why. It just was. It also was problematic. If anyone knew, especially my mother, it would be catastrophic. Way too much collateral damage for both of us. Especially for her. Her parents were the pastors of our church.

All in all, knowing all of this, I could not let her go. Our souls were tied together. Our connection was insane. Our love making was indescribable. My body experienced pleasure that I didn't know existed. My flower always jumped at the thought of it. That is what I called my vagina because it blooms when I'm aroused. My clit was the pistil and as I said it hurt every time I moved. Not in a painful way, however in a way that made me more excited.

My mom was calling me again.

"Yes, ma'am." I look up and she was standing with a handsome young man having a conversation. The young man looked familiar just couldn't place him. "Bria, I would like you to meet Duane. Duane, this my daughter Bria. She's single you know." My mother said. It took everything I had not to roll my eyes. My mom was ALWAYS doing that. Unbeknownst to her I was not available, not for him or anyone else. Of course, I would entertain her.

Well, it is nice to meet you." I shook his hand and proceeded to clean up the pews. I always had fantasies about extreme pleasure, just never thought I would be able to experience it. Never thought I could ever be this happy, that I could ever have experienced so many different forms of pleasure. At least not like this. I wish I could tell everyone how happy I was, especially my mom.

She wouldn't understand. My mom would have all the mothers of the church pray for me. I would be an abomination. I heard how she talked about Antoine who was the choir director at the church. He was clearly gay, but he was that unspoken gay. You know the type of gay I am talking about; he was clearly gay, but no one spoke about it so not to acknowledge he was gay.

If we don't speak about it clearly it doesn't exist.

My mom spoke about how ashamed his parents must be to have such a fine son and he was being wasted. How if her son were gay, she would be so ashamed that he was wasting his good genes by sleeping with men and by not having a family. How the Bible says Adam & Eve and not Adam & Steve. I tried to get her to understand it wasn't a choice and she would say everything in life is a choice. He chose men or he is just gay because he hadn't met the right woman, the one that would make him not be gay anymore. How disgusting it was for two men or two women to be together, that it was unnatural. She was even upset he was in the church, like the church isn't a house full of sinners.

I worked so hard to keep my secret. Truly wasn't easy especially because I was so in love and wanted to let everyone know. I mean I could just tell her, but she would be devastated. I could hear her now asking the Lord what she did wrong to deserve a daughter as horrible as me. Why would God condemn her with a child who couldn't give her a son-in-law and lots of grandbabies. It's always been just me and mom and I have always done what I was asked. Even went along with her little hookup dates with guys in from the church. If she knew how many of them were hoes in the church. They were sleeping with Tina, Debra, and Henrietta. Hell, anyone with a pulse and a crotch. Don't get me wrong, they were fine, just not what I wanted.

After Douglas broke my heart and started cheating with Amber, I was good. After that I really wasn't interested in the sex, and I think that was why. Douglas did not believe in foreplay and loved missionary. Also, it was way too short. I wanted to be exhausted after sex and that was not what Douglas could do. Thirty minutes later he was sleeping, and I was using my hidden toys to finish myself off.

Ha, if my mom ever found my toy stash, she would be horrified. Good girls didn't do those things. Only the weak didn't abstain from sex. She still thought I was a virgin. If she only knew half or even a quarter of the story. She would be at church on Sunday asking the pastor to baptize me again. I could see her now at the altar praying for my soul and falling out catching the Holy Ghost for her wayward daughter.

What a conundrum I am in. I really love and enjoy Stephanie. She has shown me levels of pleasure that no one else has. Unfortunately, all the years of going to church, I learned how close-minded people can be. I have heard them see transwomen and call them he/she or drag queens. You hear the whispers and the snickers and how they call all lesbians dykes. You hear the younger women what talking about how they could never eat coochie, they were strictly dickly.

From what Stephanie told me many of them had no problem getting eaten out by a woman, just didn't want anyone to know. Church folk are a funny bunch. The holiest of sinners.

Keeping secrets is never easy but sometimes it was necessary. I could not tell anyone about her. There was also no way I could control how I felt for Stephanie either. Life should not be this complicated. At night when I am home alone all I can think about is her holding me, her cuddling me. I can smell her every time I inhale and there are times, I swear I can taste her in my mouth. Stephanie has become my obsession. Every time we leave one another all I can think about is when the next time is, we will see each other again.

Every single time is new and different. Every level of pleasure is a level I have never explored. The way she runs her fingers through my hair. The touch of her hands grabbed the back of my neck. The way she just breathes me in. The level of care she shows me is hands down the best level of care I ever received. I mean my mom cares for me but with Steph it is different. It is like when I was sick and how she took a cold rag to wipe my face or how she held me when I was overwhelmed and crying. I always feel like a priority. I always feel complete. I always feel like I am enough just the way I am. She makes me feel seen and heard.

Sigh!

I wish I could share this happiness with mom, I really do. It has always been just me and mom and the church of course. My mom is not only my mom but a mother in the church also. Mom was held at the highest esteem at church and a gay/bi-sexual daughter does not fit into her image.

What would the other mothers say? What would the pastors say? On a monthly basis I heard about Sodom and Gomorrah. I heard about the evils of homosexuality. I have seen how their whispers, gossiping and lies have run Antoine's mother clear out of the church at one point. When I spoke to Antoine last, he said she hasn't even gone back to church. He said his mother felt like God abandoned her by giving her a gay son who would bring shame and ridicule to her. I honestly didn't believe that was why. When you are church enough you hear all the whispers. I think his dad was abusing him although I could not confirm. Me personally I tried to not speak with Antoine much. Call it guilt by association. Truthfully the smirk when he looks at me makes me feel like he can see my secret. Like he has a super gaydar and can smell any form of gay from miles away.

"What you over there chuckling about child?"

"Nothing ma'am just remembering a funny joke I heard." I respond.

"Care to share?" my mom responds.

No ma'am, I don't believe it is church appropriate."

"Then we shouldn't be thinking about it in church now, should we?" was her final response. I just put my head down and kept helping her clean all the mess that the church members constantly seemed to leave behind in the church pews after service. This task was so mundane, and I would prefer to be anywhere but here.

I allowed my mind to wander to when I first kissed Stephanie. We hung out quite a bit beforehand. Going to breakfast after service or just going to various church events. It was at the revival, when my mother was sick, and it was just me and Stephanie. The energy on the drive was insane. I was just drawn towards her, and I kissed her. She seemed generally shocked when I did. For a while nothing happened. In all honesty I never thought I would or could date a woman. I mean I have had experiences however never a relationship. My experiences were just heavy petting and nothing more. I knew the slightest thing about eating coochie or even being with a woman. I mean I did watch porn in secret but those were pros and without practice how would I know if I would be any good.

In the beginning Stephanie just kept things as friends. Personally, I resigned myself to thinking that it would never happen and left it at that. In my mind I would marry some good ole church boy, pump out some babies and find happiness someway, somehow. A few years back I had even pursued a girl. She was such a tease and would just keep enticing me, but it would never go anywhere. I always thought women were gorgeous creatures and just loved how they moved with their confidence. Stephanie was different.

She completely had me when months after the kiss we went for a drive. During that drive she pulled over and kissed me. It was the best kiss I ever had. That kiss made me so wet. Stephanie proceeded to put her hands in my pants. When she touched me and inhaled sharply, I turned to mush. When she dropped me off later that night, I was smitten. I couldn't get enough of her and the way she touched me, made me want her to touch me more and more. I wanted to be up under her all the time.

How could something that felt so right and beautiful be so wrong? Most importantly would I ever be able to tell my mother that I was in love with a woman?

So many questions, so few answers.

Love should never be this hard.

I am going straight to hell.

CHAPTER ELEVEN - THE BEWILDERED ONE

Stephanie

Often, I sit here at work, at my desk rubbing my fingers across my lips. Feeling her lips against mine. It would leave me with shivers like I was cold. There were times I would bite my fingers and that would make my pussy jump. I know I looked like a whole creep, and I did not care. This girl had me all the way twisted and wrapped up in my feelings.

I.... just.... did not...get...it.

Just remembering my not so long ago past. I have had some of the most beautiful women out there but there was something about Bria. She did not care that I was bi-sexual. She didn't care that I identified as gynosexual or did not conform to labels. I loved the strength of a man but preferred the softness of a woman. Just what I liked. What I wasn't a fan of was Bria was always at church. In wasn't active in the church. Well, not active in the church anymore.

I used to be a church girl like Bria until I came out to my parents. It took me fourteen years. I have known since I was like seven that I was different. I have hidden it for years. Wore all the cute Easter outfits with the lacey gloves and socks. You know with the pigtails or Shirley temple curls. Year by year becoming increasingly depressed because I didn't feel like myself. I felt like a fraud, not genuine, not living my truth. I didn't dare tell anyone with fear of being exposed for who and what I really was. The good girl makes my parents proud. Giving them a reason to brag. Following all the preset rules of being a preacher's kid. Dare I do not embarrass my pretentious parents. Well, that was until high school.

In high school there was a smorgasbord of bi-curious girls that wanted to experiment. My first experience was with a senior and I was a first-year student in the same school. She was supposed to be my math tutor. She tutored me all right, just not in math. That was an unbelievable four months until parents changed her to a geeky guy. I guess failing all of those tests was not the way to keep her. What did I know, I was only fourteen? After her it became a revolving door. The girl's bathroom became my domain. Never have to worry that someone will tell on you. Everyone had a reason to keep a secret. Especially the cheerleaders. How could they explain to their jock boyfriends they preferred my lips between their legs?

It was the perfect set up. I mean I kept a steady boyfriend at the time and would keep him at bay by sleeping with him once a month so he wouldn't ask too many questions. Then high school ended, and I went off to college.

That is where this version of Stephanie was created.

I was hoe.

A BIG HOE!!!

If the person was fine, male, or female, I was fucking them. That was until I was suspended in my junior year. That was when I was caught with my pants down literally. Got caught in a threesome with a girl and a guy. Damn shame I can't even remember their names. I'm not sure if I was more upset that the school was going to call my parents or that we were interrupted.

My parents were FURIOUS. How could I ruin their good reputation? How could they explain this if anyone found out? How could God allow them to have such a disrespectful daughter? What did they do to be given a sin for a child? Blah, Blah, Blah.

They ended up transferring me out to a college closer to home, so that they could keep their eyes on me. My parents told everyone I was homesick, so I came home. I went along with it to keep the peace plus I was running my way through the choir. If the church members knew just how freaky the choir really was. If some of the deacons had any idea on the things their wives did behind closed doors, they would be at the altar during prayer time. It was lazy of me however with my parents watching me like a hawk it was the only way I could have any fun. Especially after I moved out and shaved the side and back of my hair off.

You would have thought someone died after I cut my hair. My mother mourned my hair more than I did. My father was more upset that I didn't come to church more often after I moved away from home. Just didn't want the scrutiny or hear the judgement I heard from the church members.

Bria's mother was one of the main culprits. How she spoke about Antoine, our poor choir director, was horrid. Yes, Antoine was as gay as the day was long, but he was still human and deserved respect. Plus, there were no more eligible catches with which I hadn't already slept with. That was until I decided to go to church one Sunday and saw Bria.

It was after, I spent time together with George the night before and left with a slide. I did not entertain at my place. My place was my peace and not everyone deserved access to my peace. Also since Duane was using me as his cover-up, I never knew when he might need to stop by. The slide was decent, not the greatest, not the worst. I mean I had an orgasm or two but would not be calling her again.

Anyway, I remembered Bria. She was like eleven when I left for college. I didn't remember seeing her for a while. Believe me I would have remembered seeing her. Bria had grown up to be drop, dead gorgeous. When I said hello and hugged her, she made me start stuttering. When I started to stutter and she giggled, it was the most amazing sound to my ear. Her voice was sultry and dripped like honey. Eventually I would find out that wasn't the only thing that was like honey.

Found myself going to church more often just to run into her. How blasphemous was that. My parents were over the moon, I was in church more. Not sure how they would feel if they knew the true reason I was coming so often. I mean I still had my occasional one-night stands but there was something intriguing about Bria.

We started hanging out after church even more. Basic stuff like going to the diner to eat after service. Sometimes her mother came along but most times it was just the two of us. As I said before her mother had some amazingly strong and openly offensive things to say about gay people, so I tried to stay clear of her if I could. This thing with Bria has been going on for a few years now. It was hard to imagine what life without her would feel like.

Oh, how I remembered when it all began. It was during a revival at our mother church. Her mother asked me if she could ride with me to the revival because she wasn't feeling well and wanted Bria to go. Bria and I were just talking and heading back home, and we stopped for some fast food after the revival. I parked in the parking lot after we got our food. We ate and just kept laughing and talking. At one point we just looked at each other and SHE KISSED ME!!! I just sat here stuck and then she did it again with purpose.

Her lips tasted like honey drizzled over beignets. Her kiss left me gasping for air. Bria had caught me completely off guard. I know I said I wanted to sleep with her but usually I am the aggressor and she looked like easy prey. No one would have ever imagined that this sweet shy girl had this in her.

That was the beginning of this problematic and amazing experience. Our first time was pure magic. So much so I call her my unicorn. She did things I would have never believed she could. It was nothing short of amazing. Hard to believe she hadn't had more lovers. Maybe she was just an expert at pleasure. Ever since the beginning, each experience has been exquisite. Bria had this way of biting her lip every time she came. That was sexy as hell to me. She made me ravenous. The more she gave, the more I wanted. This always gave me a twinge of guilt. I felt like I was corrupting her. Her mother was very clear that she felt homosexuality was a sin. Ms. Harris told anyone who listened that her daughter was going to marry one of the men in the church. When I told Bria I was no good for her, she always laughed at me and told me I was being silly.

I loved Bria. Bria was amazing. She had a way of making me feel soft and vulnerable and did not judge me. We could even crack jokes during sex. It was all so easy and light although it was extremely complicated. We both vowed not to tell anyone because I was always taught that if more than two people know about a secret, it is no longer a secret. There were just too many moving pieces. Too much collateral damage for both of us if this came out. We both knew we should stop but neither of us could. It was like we were magnets just drawn to one another. After each time I saw her, I longed to be with her. I wanted to shout at the rooftops about how happy I was, just couldn't. I wasn't concerned with myself; I was concerned about her and my parents. How could I destroy everything that everyone built just for my happiness? Bria had me wanting to settle down and not want to be with anyone else. All day long I thought of her. Envisioned her kisses, the softness of her skin, the smell of her. Unsure of what I was going to do if anything at all. I wanted to see her today but couldn't. Duane was supposed to bring his son over with him today. He didn't like for him to be in the projects where he lives with his grandmother. That was another story in itself. The Duane situation was a mystery. I don't know how he was going to maneuver this one. I couldn't be concerned with his situation; I had my own.

Bria and I could talk all day long. I always wanted to pick up the phone and call her and I stopped myself because come on. I'm supposed to be a player. I'm not supposed to be doing this. Not supposed to have fallen in love. I'm not supposed to want her as much as I do, and I know Bria understands that. Things are becoming more and more complicated and that's not what I wanted, nor would I need it right now. I have enough complications faking the funk and being something I'm not. I had to wait on Bria. She was the one that dictated how this dance moved and I definitely had not had my fill of dancing in her amazing essence.

Not really a situation I could pray about. After all I have done, not sure if God even still listened to my prayers anyway. I often asked myself what was God's will for my life? After all I was still a church girl. If I could be honest God hasn't spoken to me in a long time. It didn't help that every so often my mother would say she was weeping like Jeremiah because her one and only child had lost sight of her spiritual inheritance. That I was chiding to love for myself and my immoral pleasures. Not quite sure what that meant. Last I learned God accepted all sinners who pr9ofessed that Jesus was their savior. To tell the truth, I grappled extremely hard with this. I prayed for my desires to be removed. I prayed God would deliver me. I prayed and prayed and prayed and still my desire would not subside.

What no one knew, not even Bria, was that I had a hollowness inside of me. It felt like a never-ending empty pit. It was confusing not knowing what was expected of you outside of your parents. I was always disappointing them royally and often thought that if I ended my life, it would make their life easier. The only reason I didn't was because of Bria. That was way too much onus to place on one person. She could not be the reason for my happiness or my existence. I was starting to feel like that little girl in hiding again. I wonder if I will ever get my happily ever after.

All I could do was keep praying and hoping. One thing I was going to do is keep loving Bria as long as she would have me. Even if it could only be in secret.

I'm used to it; my entire life has been in secret.

CHAPTER TWELVE - THE RESPLENDENT ONE

David

I just want to be seen.

Don't get me wrong, people see me plenty, on the surface. I want to be seen down to my core. I want someone to see my soul. Someone to see past my mask and into the core of me. Someone who will know when I am sad without me saying a word. Thought I found that person once however it was just their representative. You know what a representative is right? It is the person that shows up the first three to six weeks of a relationship. They cook dinner, buy flowers, hug & kiss. Most of all they listen and care about your concerns. Then their asses get comfortable, and all of that nice shit disappears. I have zero time or patience for any of it.

Oh well, let me deposit my check so I can pay my bills. I didn't mind the work. Although retail was a beast, being a personal shopper made it easier. Plus, being a personal shopper helped when it came time for the balls. It helped me stay on top of the upcoming fashions. I have this amazing client named Diane. Honey, she can DRESS. Every time she came in it was like she ate and left no crumbs. She applies pressure every single time she came in. I lived for her visits.

Wait did this white lady just push pass me on the line? Was this heifer trying to jump the line? I politely said "Ma'am, there is a line." Do you know what the heifer said? She said, "You people should learn to stay in your place." Excuse me. You people? She has the wrong one. I proceeded to read her to the filth that she apparently was, until those precious white tears flowed. As she cried, I stepped around her to the teller to deposit my check. Girl bye. I've been through way too much to have to deal with whatever privilege or delusion that she felt she had. There is limited to no bandwidth to deal with individual who wanted to play victim. I have all the credentials and expertise to play the lead role for that part. I have no time or patience for someone who hasn't been through 1% of what I've been through.

Life has hardened me so my willingness for foolishness is razor thin. Consider this, the last time I spoke to my parents was when my dad was throwing all my stuff out of our third-floor apartment window in the projects. He was yelling he was not raising any Aravani boys or faggots in his house. I was sixteen years old. One of my neighbors, Duane, helped me gather my stuff before the dope fiends got to it and started selling my shit. If I ever saw him again, I would thank him for his kindness because that day I needed all the kindness I could get. Where does a gay sixteen-year-old immigrant go?

I will never forget that as my dad was tossing all my stuff out like trash and calling me names Hindu and English, all the thugs were laughing. They were lucky I wasn't as petty as I am now. I would have let the entire neighborhood and their little ratchet girlfriends know, some of them have felt the warmth of my mouth and have experienced my pretty ass lips. All willingly.

I could not believe my entire life fit into one black trash bag. My entire existence was defined in that moment. Although Aravani was the name of transgender in India, I'm not transgender. Just a pretty ass gay boy. Gay Indian boy. That preferred some women's clothing. A disgrace to my family. Valued as worthless and less than. I was the reason we had to leave India. My parents got tired of defending my choices. We left late one night like we were thieves and ever since I've been disdained by my father. My mom is the sweetest, but her husband is and will always be her life. I also have two younger sisters who I love dearly. I am forbidden to speak to them or my mom. Once my dad gave a command, everyone followed.

Every now and again I would pass by the corner store that my dad owned just to see them. I walked towards the store today in hopes of a glimpse. My sister Priyanka saw me and smiled and gave a little wave and quickly went back to work. Made me both happy and extremely heartbroken. It was a melancholy existence, but I made do.

After my dad threw me out, I stayed at the Safe Haven. What a hell hole to say the least. There was minimally safe to say the least. It was safer than the streets but not my much. After 9pm the place was a free for all. I watched kids get raped and turned out all the time. There were fights almost every night.

It was to the point that the guards just gave up and let whatever happen. They would only step in when there was a chance that the violence became excessive. Most times they were basically there to finish a shift. They even tried me and failed miserably. They thought because I was a pretty ass boy, I was easy. Little did they know, I got these hands. Shit, the staff there was bullshit, and I never was or ever be anyone's bitch.

When Patrick showed up, he was my saving grace. Meeting him was the peace I didn't know I needed. We were thick as thieves. We would perform in the subways for extra funds during the day. Eventually though, I had to leave because the situation became too toxic for me. Every day going there left me depressed. I found myself not recognizing myself more and more. I was already going through issues with my identity and trying to learn to love myself.

My issue with all my good qualities I still did not feel like enough.

Patrick was sad when I left Safe Haven. He said he could never hate someone bettering themselves. I heard he ended up leaving Safe Haven shortly after I did. I tried to keep up with him but as one knows life gets in the way and you lose track of time and people for that matter. I really hope he is doing well. I will admit I do miss him. Recently I tried to find him to no success. When I left Safe Haven, I ended up staying on the streets doing whatever I needed to survive. That was all until a representative from the Ali Forney Center© came around the streets. They were out there letting us homeless gay boys know there was a place we could go. It was there I met Blair. Blair was this statuesque gay man who was a volunteer counselor at the center. Blair kept staring at me every time he saw me.

I was used to it. People always stared at me. First, I was very perplexed how fascinated Americans were with dark complexion and light eyes. I cannot tell you how many individuals commented on my "contacts" or came up and started speaking Spanish to me. It was thoroughly annoying. Second, I enjoyed wearing women's clothing. I grew so tired of explaining that although I liked women's clothing, I was ALL MAN. I wasn't trans but they always wanted to label me. I just wanted to be who I was without complications or explanations.

Over time I got to know Blair, and we forged a friendship. Eventually I found out that was the father of a ballroom house called L'Orange. He explained he had just started what is called a Kiki house. To me he might as well been speaking French. With my million and one questions, I came to find out that it was its a less prestigious house and wasn't really taken seriously the ballroom scene.

I had never been to a ball, so I went to several different ones especially to see the difference. The scene was electric and energizing. One day Blair asked me if I wanted to join his house as one of his "kids". I told Blair if I was going to compete and be part of his house, we had to be some bad bitches. I refused to waste my time with mediocrity. Been through too damn much to allow that. Blair and I worked hard to build the house for it to become a real competitor. The rehearsals were no joke. We had voguing classes, walking classes and posing classes several times a week. We worked tir9elessly to find the best of the best young talent. Went all over the city to find the best walkers, voguers, and posers. Even though Blair was older, I was the one with the gift of gab. I made those that felt all alone and abandoned welcome. We all lived in this six-bedroom house that Blair inherited from his grandfather. It was the first time in an exceptionally long time that I felt like I was part of a family. We all went out to work and lived there to assist with the bills and pay for food. All of us split the household bills and did any repairs to keep it looking good. It didn't help that the area was being gentrified. We would often get asked if we were willing to sell, which we were not. It was Blair, our father, me, our face, Devante our runway walker, Chad our labels walker, Brad our secret weapon. Brad was our Caucasian voguer, and he was beyond fierce. The girls never saw him coming. His hands were quicker than windmills. Me I walked Butch Queen Face category. I kept my face flawless and especially when everyone thought I was Spanish when I was in fact Indian was a plus. It left the judges gagging when I revealed it. Things were good until Blair passed away suddenly. He died of pneumonia which later revealed he had AIDS. He kept it a secret from all of us and I for one was devastated. During that time after Blair's death, I was lost. I went to church with my friend Antoine however it felt like judgement and damnation. Those church folks were something else. It was shocking that the men were just as bad as the women. It was just not my scene. I told Antoine I tried it and it just wasn't I think I was more devastated to know that it wasn't my cup of tea. The world judged me enough. I went there for peace and left with more judgement. I was good.

I was floored that Blair left me the house in his will. I think he did that because he knew that I would keep the house running. Once he passed, I became the new overall father of the House of L'Orange.

Working at the department store as a personal shopper helped me make sure our looks were always pristine. Through my conversations with Diane, I learned how to use key pieces to create iconic looks with a splash of flair.

We added a few more secret weapons too. There was Cassie who was our Femme Fatale, Paul who was our Transmale Realness and Paris who was our Femme Queen performer. Not only was I the overall father, but I was also their therapist and motivator. I inspired them to want more and stop boosting and get real jobs and responsibilities. I gave tough love and gave them soft love too. Wanted my kids to know I loved them, and they deserved to be here and belonged here. We fought just like real families and made up like real families too. Helped them through the relationship drama too which was a lot to say the least. We could create a gay soap opera with all the drama we encountered in this house. There is only one thing I would change if I could. I wish I could hug my mom and sisters again and remind them that I loved them. Quiet as it is kept, I wish I could hug my dad again too. Wish I wasn't such a disgrace to him and all he stood for.

Antoine James

"Everybody goes through something. You just have to be strong enough to make it through." That's what my mama said one time to me, and I will never forget it.

Originally, I was supposed to start this little book here however as you can see, they pushed a bitch to the end. So, any who, it is a pleasure to meet me I know. I am on a trip; I know but I have to be. Life has not afforded me no other alternative. How did Langston Hughes put it "Life ain't been no crystal staircase." or something like that? Oh, life has been downright tragic if you want to take that route. I will say it's been a road of unfortunate circumstances. I have been through a lifetime of pain because I "caught" the gay.

I mean I was always what they considered feminine. As a child I didn't like to be dirty and was always in the mirror fixing my face. My clothing and hair had to always be on point. Making sure each lock hair was just so. I've been a faggot for a very long time. I am what I would call an old faggot. I know, I know not the verbiage I should use however you understood exactly what I meant when I said it. It is so progressive that these young kids have so many distinctions and labels for their identities. As for me, I don't have the patience nor the inclination to try to figure out where I fit in the rainbow. I am gay, always been gay and will die gay, Periodt.

As I was saying, life has never been particularly easy. I am grateful that I am strong willed to survive or else I would be a hot ass mess. I mean my parents always knew

I was gay. They didn't necessarily approve and tried their hardest to change the behavior which was said often. See my mother always lived by the military standards. You know, don't ask, don't tell. She had to know even though she would never admit it. My mother was so happy to have a child, so she overlooked the obvious. Now as for the asshole called my dad, he refused to believe it. He thought I was gay by choice and not by design.

Damn, look at these nails!!! I needed a manicure yesterday. We have to keep ourselves looking fabulous at all times. Oh, I'm sorry I have a bit of an attention deficit and can't keep a full thought. Let me get back to my saga.

We were talking about that man called my father, right? Oh yes, anyway he thought I chose to be gay or caught the gay like it was a cold. He refused to believe his only child; his son could be gay. Quite often he tried to beat the behavior out of me. To this day I'm trying to figure out how you catch being gay. If it's a cold, can you uncatch it if you want? Is there a cure? Can I take NyQuil© and be "cured"?

Hell, truth is if someone asked, would I choose this life or catch it? The answer is No. Being gay has never been easy, not even slightly. As I was saying I was always considered feminine, and I still get a lot of slack for it. When I was younger, I was teased constantly at home, at school, at church, everywhere. I was called all kinds of derogatory names. It used to drive my father crazy. He would beat me saying "my son ain't no faggot!!!" Guess that is why I called myself a faggot. Oh, pity me.

I often wonder if when he was beating me if he ever thought about his older brother. The brother he held so near and dear when he was alive and admired so much. The brother that used to rape me for years. Who raped me from the time I was five until I was fifteen? All the while the entire time saying it was my fault because I was too pretty to be a boy. And maybe if I wasn't so feminine it wouldn't happen. Yeah, I wonder if every time he beat me if he thought of that. Funny my beatings always happened after his brother would visit. One would think my father would blame his brother for wanting to fuck his son. Probably why my uncle could never stay married. Wished I could have run and told someone. I was just too afraid that no one would believe me. Hell, when I first told my mother that is when she said that saying. If your own mother shrugged you off, what would someone else do. When my uncle finally died right before I turned fourteen, I was so happy. My father was devastated. When he died my father was all distraught and wanted me to go to the funeral. We all know that didn't happen right?? Soon after my uncle died my dad left, and it was just me and my mom. My mom apologized profusely and wanted to make amends for not protecting me. She did what she could. I forgave her but never forgot. She could have protected me better but what can one do with things you can't change? Well, the past is the past they say but in therapy I am learning that is not entirely true. The past dictates your future or in the very least that is what my therapist says. I guess some of this is true though. Otherwise, how could I justify calling myself a faggot. I guess since for years that was all I heard, I just assumed it was true. The toxicity of it all. I haven't spoken to my father's family in over 16 years. I will never forget the time I saw them. They came to the church my mother and I attended as visitors. Their looks of shock were epic. Guess they didn't expect to see my flamboyant behind directing the choir. Yes, that is right. I am the choir director at the church and am front and center EVERY Sunday. Our choir is amazing and if I do pat my own back, I am very good at what I do. I loved going to church and using my voice to praise God. What I can't stand are those damn church folk. You know the ones, holier than thou and all the while gossiping and talking about people. Even heard them saying that my mother should be so disappointed that she will never have beautiful grandbabies or that her son wouldn't be passing on his genes. Wonder what part of the Bible that was in about gossiping. Plus, isn't the church a house full of sinners in need of a savior? No one came to church just because. If I started serving the tea, many of them would be running out of the church quietly as it's kept. They are shady as fuck. Especially the ones trying so hard to turn the pastor's head. Some of the thot wear was ridiculous. If their asses sneezed their coochies would fall out. Heels so high they looked like they were walking on stilts. No need for sunglasses with all the shade they were delivering. I just grew really tired. Who I was as a person had nothing to do with me being gay? I get tired of coming to church and hearing them clicking and clucking about me and my mama. Especially one particular mother from the church. She kept saying how unfortunate it was such a waste for God to give such good looks to an abomination. Sis needed to look in her own backyard. If she had any idea of what her beautiful precious daughter was doing, she would gag. She wasn't the only one though. If some of them only knew what actually went on. A good part of my choir would rather dine at a sushi restaurant than a steakhouse, if you knew what I meant. No shade but all tea and I sip slowly. The majority of the married ones were truly pescatarian. I bet their husbands thought those big smiles were for them. They walked around peacocking like it was making them happy. Chile please. Even some of the males on the choir forgot what personal space was when they were alone with me. They were all lying and conniving. I was not in the slight bit interested. When I am in church it was all about God however when I was in the streets it was all about me. Don't judge me. God is definitely still working on me. My guardian angel was probably drunk by now based on all the mess I got into. Lol.

Folks better be lucky I am shady and not petty. Can't tell you how many times members complained to the pastors. How I was not the best representation of the church. The pastors supported it because the choir was all of that. They had people dancing and praising and the truth is more people came to the service because of the choir. This new generation loved music and music is what I do. I just hated that people condemned me without knowing my journey. My testimony would bring these people to their knees. If it hadn't been for God, Chile I can't tell you where I would be. Now don't get me wrong, I wish when I left church every Sunday, I had some companionship, but that last relationship was trash.

HOT, STINKING TRASH!!!

That chile was a beautiful creature with the ugliest soul. I was afraid if I ever brought him to church, he would catch on fire. Just pure evil for no damn reason. Met him at one of David was walking in the Butch Queen Face category. This chile was David's competition in the category. He will forever be called chile because his ass doesn't deserve a name. Any who, the boy was beautiful no doubt, but David baby was stunning. The girls tried and they always failed. David always won the category. His face was as if angels came down from heaven and kissed him from head to toe. That creature was unreal. David warned me about ole boy but nooo. Lust was stronger than reason. It was good until it wasn't, and it turned into a pure shit show. Honey this bastard tore up my good clothes, poured white paint all over my hardwood floors and cut up my damn furniture. Had to call the damn cops on him. Would you believe that the cretin had a police record longer than the seconds in a damn day? I was pissed about my stuff but praised God that he removed him out of my life. It still made me sad that I stepped over all those damn red flags and wished it would be all good. I wish I had someone to truly confide in. I had friends but none with whom I could share with. Often, I was left depressed. Left feeling like I was good enough. Like I was lacking something. After everything I've been through maybe I was too damaged to be loved. As fabulous as I appeared I felt rotten inside. I always felt out of place like something was wrong with me. I stayed prayed up, but I don't believe God is hearing me or even bothering to listen. I am going to stay praying and hoping one day God will hear me.

They say trouble don't last always but I sure wish that bitch didn't know my address anymore.

www.ingramcontent.com/pod-product-compliance
Lightning Source LLC
Chambersburg PA
CBHW030610310726
48979CB00003B/651

* 9 7 9 8 9 8 5 7 1 0 4 1 0 *